REPARATION

A TOM SCOBIE THRILLER
BOOK 2

NICK WATTS

Chiselbury

"As your member of parliament, Jed, I'm here to help you."

Tom hoped that his voice sounded nonchalant. He had inveigled himself into the home of one of the local villains, with a finger in every kind of anti-social pie he could manage.

"Oh yeah?"

Jed's response was every bit as belligerent as expected, from someone who saw himself as the kingpin of an enterprise that ran according to its own rules. He sat toad like behind a Formica topped kitchen table, whilst his MP stood like an importuning school boy before him. Tom ploughed on.

"Both you and Mr. Morris are my constituents, so think of me as a mediator."

"I think of Mister Morris as a sad loser, and you as an interfering tosser."

Jed's voice oozed contempt, seasoned with just a hint of menace. His brother, leaning against the garishly tiled wall to Tom's left, shifted his weight to remind Tom he was also there. If the purpose was to frighten, it didn't succeed. Working with a NATO mission in the Balkans, Tom had previously been part of a team tracking down local war lords, so a toe rag like this posed a manageable risk. He needed to keep his wits about him all the same. He was standing on the balls of his feet, something he learnt during his boxing training in the army. Just in case.

Tom persevered in the same emollient tone of voice. "Mr. Morris was threatening to go to the police, but I dissuaded him. I said that there could be an amicable settlement to this dispute."

Jed looked red eyed towards his brother.

" 'Ere that? Mister Morris might go to the police...." Jed's sour gaze returned to Tom.

"I make regular contributions to the policeman's charity...." He continued, as his brother laughed theatrically.

This was certainly not a regular piece of constituency case-work, Tom reflected. The brothers Smurfit were well known across the Vale of the White Horse; there wasn't a second-hand car, or dodgy building repair that didn't have their fingerprints on them. After his election just a month ago, Tom set about dealing with a backlog of constituents' case work. A chance to get to grips with the Smurfits was a chance to show them that he was different.

"Well, they might wonder at all these expensive white goods", said Tom looking around the well-appointed kitchen.

The brother reached across and picked a long kitchen knife off the bread board and began to pick at the fingernails of his other hand with the point. He was well known locally as being handy with a knife. Tom, for his part put his hands together, in front of him with the fingertips touching. He tapped his fingers together showing the brother that he was ready for anything, all the while meeting Jed's menacing stare.

"So, what's it to be?" asked Tom, with a small conciliatory smile.

Jed's complexion grew redder. Tom turned to speak to the brother.

"It's just a couple of hundred quid, what's that to you?"

The complainant Morris had bought a second-hand car off Jed, and found it was fit only for the scrap heap. This was typical of the way Smurfit did business; cash in hand and no questions asked. Any questions were usually answered with a light dusting by the brother. After which the knife came out.

"You got a nerve comin' 'ere, Scobie" Jed began to speak slowly, as if trying to restrain himself. "You're just a jumped-up farm boy."

The kitchen in the post war council house, was spacious but felt claustrophobic. A smell of stale drains, stale bodies and unwashed glasses pervaded the room. Two of them and one of him; well, he had dealt with worse odds in the Balkans. They were mostly drunken bullies and when faced with the prospect of a confrontation, backed away.

"I'm your MP, Jed – only trying to help!"

Tom had seen this technique work on his first tour of duty in the Balkans. The CO of his unit didn't take any nonsense, and made a point of confronting local troublemakers. He'd done the same, with similar results.

"I don't want any trouble, Jed. Your brother here will be a witness if anything unfortunate happens."

Before the brother could blink, Tom's reached out with his left hand and whipped the knife out of his grasp.

"What do you say?" said Tom, waving the knife towards the brother, whose expression was one of astonishment.

Jed's contempt for Tom was now directed towards his brother, who having lost face looked ashen.

"Pay the man" Jed said to his brother, in a tone more menacing than he had been using towards Tom.

Keeping his eyes on Tom and the knife, the brother reached into his windcheater pocket and fished out a bundle of blue twenties. He counted out two hundred into Tom's outstretched hand.

"Fair enough" said Tom, moving towards the back door of the house.

Pocketing the cash, he reached for the back door handle with his left hand, switching the knife to his right. As he exited, he dropped the knife onto the floor.

"Bye chaps!" he called, brightly.

Just another day at the office, he thought as he walked down the driveway. It was filled with dubious looking vans, skips and cars. He caught sight of Mike, his brother, leaning against the side of his old Land Rover. He looked relieved.

"Thought I'd have to come and sweep you up off the floor!" called Mike.

"High time those two clowns were brought down to earth" replied Tom.

Mike acted as Tom's driver when he was in the constituency, doubling as mechanic on the family farm. They got into Molly, Tom's army surplus Land Rover, so called because of the letters on the number plate MLY.

As they drove off, Tom caught sight of Jed Smurfit coming out onto his driveway. He shouted something after them as they drove past.

"Don't think they'll be voting for you, next time," said Mike.

"Put him down as a 'don't know'" replied Tom.

* * *

Weekends for Members of Parliament are the opportunity to renew acquaintance with the voters in their constituency. Local community and Party events, and a 'surgery' for constituents, are fitted in after a full week in Westminster. On a Saturday lunchtime Tom was weaving his way through a merry gathering of the party faithful, in a large chalk block farmhouse at the foot of the Downs. It was a fine spring day. Many were there to see their new MP for themselves.

"Very good of you to come, Tom", his host's voice was a conspiratorial whisper amidst the hubbub. He was leading him through the crowd, to meet the Ward Chairman. One or two of those gathered gave him the sort of look that reminded him that he was not everybody's first choice of candidate.

"A couple of bandits here", said Tom.

His host, a kindly man with a farmer's wind-blown face, looked at him blankly. He knew little of the behind-the-scenes shenanigans which had led to Tom being elected after the unexpected death of the previous incumbent.

"Paid up members of the Charles Markham appreciation society" Tom explained. Markham had maintained a network of supporters in the area, bolstered by the use of his patronage. Now he was in prison and Tom had helped to put him there.

Tom wasn't sure whether his host's lack of reaction was embarrassment, or puzzlement. He was led towards the end of a well-proportioned sitting room, with large picture windows that allowed plenty of spring sunlight in.

The gathering was a fund-raising event, the sort of occasion that punctuates the life of every MP. Tom had got used to the sort of small talk that these occasions required. Every now and again, someone would button hole him on a particular issue. For this he carried a small notebook in his jacket pocket.

"Good to see you Tom!" the genial voice of the Ward Chairman boomed. "I see you're equipped with a drink", he added.

The Ward Chairman was a City banker, who affected a style of dress that suggested a country squire. His chief virtue, in Tom's eyes, was that he was not one of Markham's bandits.

"How's the family these days?" he asked, by way of polite chat.

"Growing!" replied Tom with a smile. "If your wife is a doctor, you spend your whole life having symptoms, especially when you're expecting a *wee'an*."

"A few choice words, Tom!" suggested the Ward Chairman. "Then we'll get onto the raffle".

After his speech and the excited hubbub of the raffle, Tom was happy to re-fill his glass and relax a little. He saw someone who looked like a button-holer come into view, and fished his note book out of his pocket, in readiness.

"You don't have to write this down Mr. Scobie" he began in a pleasant voice, "I've got a message from a mutual acquaintance."

Tom didn't recognise him as one of the bandits, but he was instantly alert. His demeanour wasn't threatening, but his message was.

"You've been fortunate, Mr. Scobie, but you need to stay lucky!" With that he turned and walked back into the crowd. The Ward Chairman, who had been chatting to another guest, saw that Tom's expression had changed.

"All well Tom?"

"Who was that?" asked Tom. Peering into the crowd, the Ward Chairman pulled a face.

Glancing to his right, Tom noticed a French window open to allow air to circulate. Handing his glass to the bemused Chairman, he walked briskly out through the window and ran around to the area where the cars were parked. He was just in time to see a four-by-four pull away. The profile of the driver resembled the messenger. He caught sight of the registration; that would be a useful lead to explore.

"I think your luck just ran out, matey" he said to himself. He tried to make a mental note of the face. You never knew when you might bump into someone.

The host had followed Tom and walked up to join him.

"Do you know who drives that car?" Tom said, pointing to the retreating four by four.

"Er, not really, might've been a friend of one of the members. Tickets were on general sale", he said. Tom thought better of making too much fuss, and they both turned back towards the house.

"A very good crowd you managed to gather" said Tom, changing both the topic and the mood.

"A pleasure, Tom" replied the host. "I was in the Young Farmers with your dad. So, if there's anything I can do, er, to help....."

Tom made a mental note to send him a nice thank you, maybe a card from the Palace of Westminster. He also made a note to contact Georgina and her team of investigative journalists to see who the mystery messenger was. He would then send a message, right back to Markham.

2

After the morning's event Tom sat in Molly and called Georgina, relating the brief encounter. She said she'd get her bunch of citizen journalists, who she called her elves, on to the case. He knew that he'd get a lead swiftly, but he didn't ask how the information was obtained.

"Markham is the gift that keeps on giving" she said wearily. She had taken over the journalistic investigation into Markham and his cronies, after the death of Jack Sawyer. It was Jack who had approached Tom with information about Markham's network; his 'accidental' death persuaded Tom that his work should be pursued. Between them they had managed to obtain enough evidence to get Markham arrested and make his constituency agent and others flee to Northern Cyprus, to avoid being arrested.

"I suppose it was too much to hope that he'd take his medicine like a good boy" Tom said, trying to inject some levity into the proceedings.

"After having his empire dismantled and lost his house into the bargain, he's looking to restore his *amour propre*" replied

Georgina. "He's obviously still got a few friends in the Vale of the White Horse" she added.

"I had a feeling that he might be able to reach out from behind the bars" Tom said almost to himself. "I might see if I can bump into one of my ministerial colleagues and ask a few questions."

"I bet you we get some good info before too long, Tom" came the reply, almost relishing the challenge. They ended the call and Tom then drove to the constituency office in Wandage. He enjoyed a few minutes of privacy as he drove Molly through the country lanes which were burgeoning in the spring weather. But he was watchful as he drove.

"Hello Mu" he called to Muriel Makepeace, the office manager cum constituency agent who was presiding over a motley crew of volunteers in the garret-like office.

"How was it?" she asked, bustling about the small office.

"Good" replied Tom, to keep it short. This was not the time for a long conversation. Time with the MP at the weekend was precious, so down to business, thought Tom. For an hour they went through a list of invitations to events across the constituency and looked at some constituents' request to attend his next 'surgery' where they would bring their complaints about bureaucracy or their neighbours. As he walked over to the coffee pot his phone rang. It was Georgina. He waved to some of the departing volunteers as he listened.

"We've got something on someone who has been visiting His Lordship in prison recently." As ever she was all business. "Some work we've been doing to keep a track of his cronies."

"Remind me never to get on the wrong side of you!" said Tom. He was gratified to hear Georgina laugh. Jack's death cast a shadow over everything she did; Tom had cautioned her not to let it eat her up.

"I've also got some news about the elusive Mr. Johnson".

Donald Johnson acted as Constituency Agent for the Ridgeway constituency. He had fallen under Markham's influence and acted as his fixer. Somehow he had got wind of the net closing in on the Markham enterprise and disappeared, turning up in Northern Cyprus where he was safe from extradition.

"Up until now, Johnson has been holed up in Kyrenia. Various types come and go, and they seem unconcerned about being spotted" she added. "Recently he has managed a few sorties around the region, with the help of friendly border officials, to Lebanon and Transdnistria in Moldova."

"Holidays from Hell" mused Tom.

"I think it means he is up to something" she added.

"By the way, I've passed on the details of the car you gave me; I'll get the elves working on it." They ended the call. Georgina's network of citizen journalists would be looking out for the vehicle concerned and report in. She didn't trust the police, or private detectives, who were usually ex-coppers. Information was power, she kept reminding her team.

Tom gestured for Muriel to walk with him into his inner office and he gave her the details of the conversation. He also related his earlier encounter. Muriel's husband Henry had fallen foul of Markham's malevolent plans. Despite all, Muriel and Henry had rallied to help Tom win the election, only for Henry to be revealed as another of Markham's stooges. Mu had been heartbroken to discover his treachery. It was she who urged Tom to stand whilst Henry had played along.

"He obviously feels safe enough moving around. Perhaps he's getting cabin fever" said Tom, so as to draw out Muriel's own reaction.

"Springtime in the Levant and the Balkans?" she asked whimsically. "A lovely time to go travelling!"

Her expression gave the lie to the levity of her remarks. Life had returned to a semblance of normality in the sleepy Vale of the White Horse. Tom's encounter this morning reminded them both that this could prove to be a false hope.

"We crack on, Tom!" she said, putting a lid on any negative thoughts.

Tom took the hint.

* * *

"Georgina's on the case, Sid, but I'd like you to see what you can discover around the bazaars." Tom was back at Shepherds Cottage, their home at the foot of the Downs. Considering that it had once been the home for a family with four children in the 1950s, it seemed rather luxurious to have been just the two of them. Then, as he was staring a new life, a little one was expected, as an early Christmas present for them both.

"Roger that" replied Sid with his usual laconic voice. "Just look after your lovely lady Pathfinder." Tom and Sid had served together in the reconnaissance platoon in the same regiment. Despite leading a patrol into a village belonging to a hostile militia in Bosnia, Sid had stuck with him when he was asked to join a taskforce pursuing war criminals. The ironic nickname had stuck.

"Georgina's team has a list of names of those who have been visiting Markham in prison, so there may be a few friendly faces we can pay a call on", suggested Tom.

"I'll make sure to give the matter my full attention along with my other commitments." Tom could hear the smile in Sid's voice. Since leaving the army he had managed to find work by word of mouth and didn't lack for clients.

As they ended the call, Tom heard the sound of Anna's car pulling on to the gravel driveway. "Hellooooo" she called over her shoulder. Tom decided that this was not the moment to share the latest developments with Anna. She had been through a lot during the election campaign, as Markham tried to use her colourful past life as a lever to blacken Tom's name. She had also avoided an acid attack from Markham's protégé who had gone mental after losing the selection.

"What time did we ask Matt and Lizzie to arrive?" asked Anna as she passed Tom groceries for him to put away.

"Six-ish" he replied reaching up to a high cupboard.

Tom's cousin Matt was one of the few people he felt really comfortable with. He had been like an elder brother to Tom despite having three of his own. He and Matt saw the world the same way. Lizzie, his wife, had been enthusiastic about Anna when he took her to meet them. "She'll keep your feet on the ground, Tom!" she had said - and she was right. He smiled at the recollection.

3

"Trust nobody."

The conspiratorial tone of his companion caught Tom's attention. He was one of the 2010 intake of MPs being entertained in the ornate Speaker's House in Westminster. The elegant, panelled room was full of excited newbies. He gave him an appraising look as he took a sip from his wine glass. The other one continued.

"The leader of our great party couldn't manage to defeat an unpopular government without forming a coalition", he continued.

"There are a lot of unhappy bunnies in this party. They'll be looking to de-rail his plans or remove him."

He was speaking of the Prime Minister recently installed. It's a little premature to be thinking of a change of leadership, thought Tom.

"I'll keep my powder dry and my flints sharp" replied Tom, non-committaly.

Already learning to dissemble, he thought: Welcome to Westminster.

"Gentlemen, welcome to you both!"

The genial tones of Mr. Speaker cut through the hubbub as he circulated. It was Tom's turn for attention. A cheery handshake and he moved on.

"Roger Burnside, by the way" his companion added, in a manner that suggested a previous life in the City of London.

Roger Burnside had won a seat somewhere in outer Essex in Constable country. His round face was already flushed from drinking Mr. Speaker's wine. Tom saw his gaze fall upon a young lady on the opposite side of the room who was talking to a male MP.

"You have no friends here, Tom; this place is a snake-pit", Burnside added. How he had come to this conclusion after such a short time in Westminster was something Tom could only guess at.

"Damsel in distress" said Roger, giving Tom a grin. "Got to rescue her from that tedious prat" he said, nodding towards the pair.

Tom watched as he wove his way unsteadily across the room through the throng. He found a passing waiter and helped himself to another glass. He allowed his gaze to wander over the portraits of former Speakers that adorned the panelled walls. The evening light from the tall windows illuminated the gilt ornamentation of the wood panelling. Not a bad place for a booze-up, he thought.

"He's not called Roger for nothing" came a stage-whispered voice as a hand reached for a glass off another tray as it passed.

Tom turned to his left and saw a smiling face with a bright pair of dark eyes.

"Kathleen Quinlan – Kat" she introduced herself.

"Labour Co-op for Nottingham South-West" she added.

Tom introduced himself in similar vein.

"Ah! Midsomer Murders." She referred to the TV programme with an improbably high murder rate.

"There was a story about you after the election. How several people had, er, nasty accidents.".

Tom couldn't judge whether she was being amusing or trying to draw him out. Either way he felt he ought to defend the honour of the Vale of the White Horse.

"There were some bad apples who had to be exposed" he began.

"And what about the fire at your house?" she continued. "You're at the southern end of our regional telly, so I saw it on the local news."

Tom gave a quick explanation of events in Ridgeway after his adoption to contest the seat. He sensed that Kat was a friendly sort, and life in Westminster meant making friends wherever you could find them. She blanched when Tom told her of the attempted acid attack on Anna.

"Poor duck - she alright?"

Tom nodded as he took another sip.

"She's a tough highlander. Not only did she get to redecorate the house but she announced that she was pregnant too!"

Kat looked at him as he spoke and smiled.

"You're a big softy really! All that Captain Fantastic stuff they said about you. I could see your eyes welling up, mister."

Tom couldn't hide his smile.

"I'm a very lucky man" he said.

Kat gave him a nod to signify that all was understood.

"Watch your back, Tom" she said. "In my experience, the people who did that often have friends. Now that you're in here, they'll try to bring you down."

* * *

As the business jet banked over the Black Sea, Donald Johnson allowed the bright evening sunshine to play on the champagne in his glass. He felt that, at last, he was back in the game.

"Follow me through passport control, Mister Marsh," said Darren, his associate, referring to the alias on Johnson's passport.

"Immigration has been squared away" he added, giving him a knowing look.

"This has a good feeling about it" said Donald, glancing at the sparkling champagne flute.

"I'm talking about the meeting, not the fizz!" he added.

The business jet descended from the clear blue sky and made a discreet landing at Varna airport. A Black Sea resort, Varna was enjoying a renaissance after Bulgaria joined the European Union. Tourists came for the beach, especially from Russia and the eastern members of the EU, who had travelled there in 'former times'. Varna was also a magnet for 'investors' and 'businessmen' looking to profit from the new hotels and beach resorts and - more importantly for Don and Darren - the casinos.

For Donald Johnson this was both an enjoyable excursion from his self-imposed exile in Northern Cyprus (where he was safe from extradition to the UK) and a chance to spread his wings and re-invigorate the business interests that he was involved in on Markham's behalf. He saw himself as an old-school business buccaneer for whom rules were useful as long as they suited his purpose. He was taking a leaf out of the book of his mentor Lord Charles Markham, except that Markham had become careless and had fallen foul of the law. He wouldn't make the same mistake.

The small party walked across the apron in the warm sunshine and into the cool of the terminal building. He handed over the passport with a confident smile. The official behind the glass screen gave it a cursory glance and handed it back. UK passports needed no visas to enter the country and vice versa.

"The drive to the Sunny Sands resort won't take long but we'll enjoy the scenery as we ride", said his companion.

They were re-united with their bags which Dimitar their concierge had taken through customs. As they walked out to the waiting car Donald began to quiz Darren; he liked to know who he was dealing with.

"These boys have managed to get a good slice of the business here and they're looking to add some value to their endeavours. That's where we come in."

The summary was commendably brief. "We'll supply the girls, booze and fags. They'll handle the gambling and the drugs."

"Complementary activity" observed Donald, opening the door to the waiting Mercedes.

"The joys of a Single Market and a passport-free zone," said Darren. "Once we've got the girls registered here they can get around much more easily. Once the rest of the Balkans joins the EU we'll be all over it!"

"Well, we'd better be nice to our new friends" echoed Donald.

"In my experience" he continued "there are always little jealousies among these folks. Usually about respect as much as money. We just have to work out who hates who the most, and we can play them like puppets."

4

"**M**orning, Scobie!" came a voice, as he started down the stairs. Looking behind him Tom saw James Green, a veteran MP for a Wiltshire constituency.

"How's tricks?" Green enquired jovially. After a short time in Parliament Tom had got used to the Westminster practice of conducting conversations on the run between engagements, so kept his reply brief.

"On my way to the FAC" referring to the Foreign Affairs Committee. "You?" "Defence Committee" came the equally terse reply.

The Committee Hearing Rooms were two floors down, so they soon reached the first floor of Portcullis House, where they went their separate ways. Portcullis House is a modern annex of the House of Commons on the opposite side of the road to the Palace of Westminster. Tom was able to slide into his seat as the chairman was making his introductory remarks.

His thoughts wandered as he opened his folder. Amongst his papers he found an envelope. The handwriting was Anna's. He decided to wait until later before opening it. She had developed the trick of slipping cards and notes into his bag before he left their house. Now she had mischievously suborned Amy his PA into the process. He smiled to himself.

"Likes the sound of his own voice......" His neighbour Kat, the Labour MP from Nottinghamshire who he'd met at the Speaker's House reception, mumbled conspiratorially to avoid being heard. She leant towards him. The Chairman's opening remarks were beginning to drag on. They were both sitting at one end of a horseshoe-shaped table in a square committee room with lots of glass and modern art works on the walls. Tom tried to suppress a smile. Despite coming from different political tribes, MPs on a Select Committee quickly form friendships across the ideological divide.

"The sky is blue, the grass is green" Tom responded in kind. Unfortunately he had leant forward a little too far and his voice was picked up by the directional microphone on the desk. His comments were broadcast around the room and to the audience watching the live feed on TV.

"I'll get to you shortly, Mr Scobie." The chairman looked peeved, while some of the others on the committee were also smiling. The incident would help to bolster Tom's reputation as a free thinker after unexpectedly securing the candidacy in a very safe seat.

"The Honourable Member for Ridgeway is obviously dying to start proceedings....." The chairman's introduction over, he had thrown the ball in Tom's direction. He looked at the chairman and smiled his thanks before turning towards the witnesses. His mind went blank as to who the three stooges sitting at the witness table were. He hoped that his demeanour was nonchalant as he began to parrot something about adding his own welcome to the witnesses and thanking them for sparing the committee their time. All the while he was looking out his memo for the meeting. Found it – he looked down at his notes and launched into his opening question.

* * *

"How do you see things, Tom?" Sitting in the atrium of Portcullis House reminded Tom of a bazaar in the Middle East with its hubbub of noise. Everybody was here to exchange gossip or information. It put him in mind of his work in the Balkans where he was part of a NATO taskforce trying to understand the links between rival militias and criminal gangs.

"I don't think anybody foresaw the advent of a coalition just as they didn't foresee the economic crash. But we have to do our best to remember the people who sent us here and why." He could see that the lobby journalist sitting opposite him was nonplussed by the answer. In politics knowledge is power, so any snippet of information was valuable to journalists seeking a story.

He had been warned about Gordon Pugh, a muckraking lobby journalist, so Tom chose his words with care.

"I'm relatively new to this game, so I'm flying by the seat of my pants – sorry if that's unhelpful!" He had had plenty of deal-ings with local journalists after he was elected and had worked closely with an investigative reporter who was looking into the death of his predecessor. He understood that journalists have a job to do, reporting on what politicians get up to.

"As a backbencher I am meant to represent my constituents and use my judgement to scrutinize the government, as we were doing in the Foreign Affairs Committee this morning."

"How was the minister?" probed Gordon.

"He played a dead bat" replied Tom. "It's too early into a new government for anything of significance to emerge. It was just a *tour d'horizon*."

Tom was seen as something exotic in Westminster - someone with no political baggage - so perhaps the journalist was hoping for some indiscretions or disparaging comments. An uneasy coalition had been cobbled together after the election and plenty of MPs from both parties were unhappy about it. Tom was just happy to have been elected.

"Ask me after I've been here a year" he said.

He continued chatting with the journalist for as long as it took them to finish their coffee. Gordon then made his excuses and went in search of more productive quarry. He looked at his watch: nothing for half an hour - bliss. He closed his eyes. It had already been a long day. A working breakfast was followed by the FAC session and then the meeting with the journalist. Yesterday evening went on too late and he struggled through his morning run in to the office. And it was only Tuesday.

"Hello, sleepy!" Amy's voice brought him back to the present. He groaned theatrically and looked up to see the slight figure of his young PA smiling at him quizzically. He had recruited her when Parliament returned after the election. She had previously worked for an MP who had retired. She had no connection with his predecessor or with any of the troubled history that went with him.

"Some spooky woman has come to the office looking for you" she said, her expression suddenly serious. Members of the public could not get into the building without passing through security and being escorted whilst on the premises.

"How did she get in?" he asked. Amy shrugged. He was still on the alert after his run-in with a contract killer hired by Lord Markham who had been responsible for a string of deaths in the run-up to the election. Amy was sensible and knew the story. Perhaps this was the emissary he'd been told to expect when the PM contacted him just after he'd won the election.

"She seems OK, she's got a pass. I left Fred to look after her." Fred was an intern gaining work experience whilst studying at King's College London. They walked over to the lift and took it to the third floor. Tom led the way into the office where Fred was tapping away at his computer. He looked up and nodded towards the adjoining office where Tom's desk and coffee table were.

"How do you do?" said Tom coolly walking into his office. He decided to let her do the talking. He put his papers onto his desk. Amy hovered by the door waiting to see if any coffee would be needed.

"Do please excuse the intrusion, Mr. Scobie" she began. "I wasn't sure where to find you."

She was neat with short brown hair, wore a dark jacket and trousers and had a concerned expression. Civil servant, thought Tom; this lady wasn't a killer. She could be from the security adviser's office, an ex-spook who oversaw arrangements for Members' safety among other things. He had met Tom when he arrived to discuss his 'circumstances'.

"Mr. Evans would like to see you at your earliest convenience" she continued, confirming Tom's suspicions. "Later today, perhaps?" she said. "This does not concern recent events in your constituency or your personal safety" she added, giving Amy what was meant to be a reassuring smile.

They agreed on a 2:30 meeting in Mr. Evans' office.

Well, well, thought Tom - what was this all about?

5

"Thank you for seeing me, Mr Scobie" said Evans as Tom entered his functional office in one of the parliamentary buildings set away from the Palace of Westminster. Tom saw that he was not alone. A suave-looking man in his mid-thirties was also in the small office, making the place claustrophobic.

"Adam" he said, introducing himself. Tom noted the spooks trick of not using surnames, so what was going on?

"How can I help?" He decided to cut to the chase. Evans gestured for them all to sit and ordered some coffee. This then was what the PM had been speaking about. Adam pulled a photograph from a folder he was carrying and handed it to Tom. As Tom studied the face, he began to explain.

"You might recognise this chap Nikolay Todorov?" Adam watched Tom's face for any sign of recognition.

"You were at school together" he suggested helpfully.

"He's put on a bit of weight! Yes – we called him Toddy" said Tom looking up.

"Went back to Bulgaria after 1989 to reclaim his family property" continued Adam. "Quite the tycoon these days. He has political ambitions but he seems to have made friends with some shady characters. He's coming over with a delegation next week. We'd be grateful if you could re-acquaint yourself with him? I'm sure he'd be pleased to meet an old classmate, especially one who is now an MP".

Tom let the idea sink in, while feeling a familiar tingling sensation. This was something like the work he had done in the Balkans so not exactly new to him. He'd described his previous work to Anna as 'talent spotting and baby-sitting' which was a rough approximation of his work. He had left out the more menacing elements. He realized that his past activities would be well known to people in the security world. He needed time to think, before committing himself either way.

"Is the idea to recruit Toddy?" he asked.

"We'd like to learn a little bit more about him and his associates" replied Adam. "We can't judge whether he's gone rogue or simply got himself in with a bad bunch. He has dual nationality so any criminality could land him in hot water, both here and in Bulgaria."

Tom was conscious that Evans was watching him with the expression of a friendly schoolmaster. He stirred himself to speak, glancing at Adam as he did so. "You'll recall Tom that the remit of the....security services, these days includes organised crime not just old-fashioned espionage", he glanced at Adam before continuing. "Bulgaria has joined the EU much against the wishes of some member states, but it was felt politically expedient to have them inside the tent so that we could assist them with their, erm, reform efforts."

"Cleaning up the place?" suggested Tom. He was rewarded by nods from the others.

"Todorov has got himself connected to some EU-funded projects in which the UK government has a financial interest" continued Adam. "We need to understand where the money is going as we think it may be being siphoned off by organised criminals."

"Do you want me to warn him off?" asked Tom, still trying to decide if he wanted to re-enter his old world, even briefly.

"Not yet" replied Adam. "We want to understand the network and the extent of his involvement in it." Sounds familiar, thought Tom. His efforts to understand the extent of Markham's web of influence was one factor in his deciding to stand for the nomination - and look where that had got him. Besides he enjoyed the game.....

"Are you looking for a prosecution?" asked Tom. He was suddenly struck by the thought that Toddy could find himself in deep trouble. "That may be a question for the CPS" responded Adam.

Tom pulled a face. The Crown Prosecution Service had a chequered record at securing convictions and Tom worried that they might be looking for an easy target. He would have to use his judgement on how to handle Toddy once he had the full picture.

"OK, if you can give me a brief I'll see what I can do to help."

"All covered by the Official Secrets Act, Tom", said Evans, bringing him back down to earth.

* * *

"Is this more boy scouting, Tom?" Anna's expression was neutral. She knew about the PM's phone call.

Back home at Shepherds Cottage on Thursday evening, Tom and Anna were catching up on the events of the week. Anna was aware of Tom's previous life in military intelligence which she referred to as boy scouting. He had put some of his tradecraft to work in his efforts to uncover the Markham network. She was glad that his knowledge of the dark arts had kept them safe despite Markham's best efforts.

"It's nothing too spooky, just the chance to catch up with an old schoolmate" he said in what he hoped was a reassuring tone. "I could just stop him going to jail if I can send the right message" he added as an afterthought.

Anna saw the sense of this and nodded as the thought sunk in.

"It's just...." she began.

"Hmmm...?" He knew her moods well enough to know that she was unhappy.

"Just remember that there are now three of us in this marriage!"

"I know we've been through a lot, *I* put you through a lot" he continued as he pulled her towards him and enfolded her in his arms.

"It only drew us closer, made us stronger" she said her voice muffled by his embrace. "Besides, you're smarter than they took you for!"

Not for the first time, Tom wondered how on earth he had been so lucky as to find such a free-spirited creature who had accepted him unconditionally. Markham had seen Anna as his weak flank, but beneath her other-worldliness she had a core of pure steel.

"So, tell me about this rogue" she said as she disengaged herself. She poured him a glass of wine and a glass of elder-flower for herself, now that she was with child. She brought them over to the big refectory table at the heart of their kitchen. Tom fished out some crisps from a shelf and they both sat down.

"Toddy we called him at school" he began. He spoke about a big boy who was always a bit of an outsider. He wanted to be liked and was good at sports; later in life he went into property development where he seemed to do quite well. "After 1989 the new Bulgarian government undertook a programme of restitution to return property confiscated by the communists. I'd heard that Toddy went back to Varna where his family came from originally" he explained.

"Didn't you go to Bulgaria?" Anna remembered one of his tales.

"Yes - to Plovdiv and then Dobrich, pursuing some dodgy characters" he recalled. He was part of a NATO task force led by the British general for whom he was initially an ADC. Tom had been talent-spotted by his boss 'Lucky Jack' Jones and put to work with the task force. Part of his role was to identify 'bad guys' and pursue them in search of evidence to arrest them. One such character had a regular meeting in Plovdiv with Russian gangsters. The Russians were beyond his remit; his target was a Bosnian Serb.

"And this chap is swimming with these sharks!?" Anna sounded intrigued.

"I'll use all of my charm to put him at his ease and get to the bottom of what he's got involved with" Tom said as he pulled some crisps from the bag. Although his grandfather encouraged him to look for the best in people when he was a young boy running around the farm, experience had taught him that even good people can be drawn into bad places either through weakness or by making bad choices.

"Sounds good to me" Anna said, taking a sip from her glass. Tom was relieved that her worries were set aside for now.

Tom stared at the light reflected in his wine glass. Markham's network had been mixed up in the Balkans among other things. Was Nikolay connected somehow? It was unlikely but the criminal gangs in that part of the world operated on tribal and family lines. Somebody might know somebody; a favour here, a vendetta there.

"You never know what might emerge if you kick some stones around" Tom said, almost to himself.

6

"Tomeee!" The distinctive voice cut through the throng as Tom mingled with other guests in the splendid setting of the Guildhall in the City of London. Tom looked in the direction of the voice and recognised Toddy coming his way with a hand outstretched.

"Well, look at you!" Tom's smile was genuine as he saw his old schoolmate.

"Small world" replied Toddy as they shook hands warmly.

The group of Bulgarians had been invited by the Corporation of London to a dinner to meet potential investors and other British dignitaries. Their visit had been jointly put together by the Government (keen to promote the UK as an investment centre) and the Bulgarian Government, also keen to promote Bulgaria as a place to do business. The group was led by a Bulgarian Government minister.

"I saw your name on the list" began Toddy. "There can't be too many Tom Scobies in the world!"

Tom had persuaded Adam the spook that this first meeting should be a chance to catch up on old times and to understand what Toddy was up to. The group was due to visit the House of

Commons later on during their visit so a follow-up meeting should be easy to arrange; at which point Tom could start digging.

"Congratulations by the way!" said Toddy grabbing another glass from a waiter, "I saw that you'd been elected. I never had you down as a politico." Tom shrugged. 'Right place, right time' was the way he'd summed up his change of direction since his election.

"Good move!" said Toddy as he looked around him at the splendour of the Guildhall. "I like this place...." Tom caught a glimpse of unalloyed enjoyment on Toddy's face. 'I've arrived' it seemed to say.

"I never got to go to a place like this before I went back to Varna" he began. "Just wet holidays in Devon!" He smiled at Tom recalling former times. Tom noticed that Toddy liked to talk possibly through nervousness, which would make questioning him easier.

"How's it going?" A nice open question, which enabled Toddy to tell Tom of his success in the property business in Bulgaria. Another glass of wine, and he was well into his life story as they were all ushered into dinner.

* * *

A reception at the Speaker's House in the Palace of Westminster was arranged for the group the evening before they departed. Tom invited Toddy to dinner afterwards in the Strangers' dining room.

"Look at this place, Tommy!" Toddy was wide eyed in admiration. "High Victoriana" replied Tom trying not to appear too nonchalant. The Strangers' dining room looked out on to the river and the wood panelling and carpet gave the place the air of a mid-county's restaurant.

"When Britain was at the height of her power..." Toddy was unabashed in his admiration. "A nice place to eat!" he said, smiling at Tom as if congratulating him on having landed a plum position.

"Have you had a useful visit?" Another open question which allowed Toddy to impress Tom with a run-down of all the potential investors he had spoken to. People keen, so he thought, to invest in his beach front project in Varna.

"How different is it from property development here?" Tom knew that Toddy had followed his father into the property business after leaving school.

"Much less red tape but plenty of....*bureaucracy!*" Tom gave him a quizzical look, which elicited a fuller explanation of how to succeed in the property business in Bulgaria. What Toddy was describing seemed to be about ensuring he got the right permits and the right people to work on the projects he ran.

"Property without infrastructure is just empty space" he added. "I'm looking at a venture involving some EU finance, which will connect us to the airport and modernize the local waste disposal!" Ah ha! thought Tom. Now we're getting somewhere.

At that moment, the division bell rang. Other MPs in the dining room got up to head towards the division lobby. "Don't go away!" said Tom, as he joined the others on their way to vote.

"What's the vote this time?" he asked a colleague. "Dunno – just do what the whips say..." came a befogged response. Someone's having a good dinner, thought Tom.

* * *

"How do you feel about a trip to the sunny Black Sea, Anna?" Lizzie's voice rang across the kitchen.

Tom's cousin Matt and Lizzie his wife were two of the people

Tom and Anna felt most comfortable with. Matt had left a life in corporate marketing for a new role as a vicar but had become involved in the reconciliation and mediation area. Tom always introduced him as Terry Waite's younger brother. Matt understood Tom, because their careers seemed to mirror each other's.

"Right now, I'd be happy just to sit in the garden, and catch up on the stack of books I've got to read!" replied Anna, making a show of putting her hands on her baby bump which was still quite small.

"The invitation has been extended by my former classmate who is a property magnate in Bulgaria" explained Tom. During their dinner together Toddy had suggested that he and Anna should spend some of their summer holiday at his villa in Varna. At his de-brief with Adam from the Security Service the following morning, this suggestion was discussed. Tom wanted to check with Anna who was not enjoying her pregnancy. Anna pulled a face which Tom understood as a 'no'. "If this is work you'd be best on your own" she had said.

"It's fine, Anna" said Lizzie "there's plenty that us girls can get on with while Tom is playing buckets and spades on the beach!" Matt was the only person who knew about this new dimension to Tom's career as an MP. He had invited himself and Lizzie over so that they could speak about it the weekend after Tom had met Toddy. "So this chap is doing quite well for himself?" he ventured as they were getting Saturday brunch ready.

"Looks like it" said Tom as he laid the cutlery on the table. "He has the air of someone who wants to impress you. Look at me – how great I am, that sort of thing."

"A bit too naïve?" suggested Matt. "This might lead him into situations where he could be manipulated by others, using him as a fall guy."

"Also" he continued "you need to remember the Balkan

culture of obligation. His responsibility will be to his family and the extended clan he belongs to. Any western considerations of what we call fair play will be replaced by what people expect him to do for them."

"What did spooky guy say?" asked Anna as she brought the coffee pot over to the table. "Have you got a plan?"

Having laid the table Tom was now on toast duty. "We think that if I went to see him on his own turf it might help us understand whether Toddy is a criminal, or whether he is being too reckless. But if he's using money from the British taxpayer via EU funds, then he needs to be warned about his behaviour."

"Besides" he added "the invitation is for a weekend gathering, so it'll be interesting to see who he keeps company with.

7

S itting in the office of Mr Evans the parliamentary security officer with Adam from the Security Service, Tom was going over the plan for his next engagement with Toddy. He had agreed to attend the party Toddy was throwing just after Parliament rose for the summer recess. Tom had explained to Toddy that Anna would not be accompanying him owing to her condition.

"This is still very much first impressions," said Adam. "We'd like your take on who his associates are, how they live and where the money comes from."

"The good news is that Toddy isn't shy about bragging" replied Tom. "When we met he couldn't wait to tell me what a success he was." He saw both Adam and Mr Evans nod their understanding. "That could be helpful," said Adam. "Just lead him gently."

"When he's had a drink or two his guard drops, so I'll let him get relaxed before probing further" said Tom. "I remember the technique – open-ended questions."

"How are you travelling, Tom?" asked Mr Evans. "This isn't parliamentary business."

Tom smiled. "Budget travel!" They all laughed. "Flight to Sofia and connect to Varna. Toddy will send a car to collect me at the airport."

"Very neat" said Adam.

* * *

"I've forgotten how hot it can be here!" said Tom, as the car pulled away from Varna airport. "Thanks for coming – I thought you said you'd send a car...."

"Well, I can't allow an old school chum to miss out on the sights and sounds of my home town!" Toddy powered the Mercedes onto the main road and soon they were heading north along the coast. The combination of sun and sea and new development gave Tom the impression of any Mediterranean resort - except this was the Black Sea coast.

"In the old days the families of the high-ranking party officials came here" explained Toddy as he drove at high speed. "Now we are democratising the place. Anyone can come as long as their money is good!"

They continued along the coast road past a few semiderelict cottages which were in contrast to the new developments being built closer to the beach. After about ten minutes Toddy drove the car up a driveway lined with bushes and trees of varying heights which led to a villa, surrounded by an English-style lawn. The land sloped gently giving a view over the sea.

"Wow!" said Tom; his reaction was genuine.

"My family house" explained Toddy. "Taken by the communists and given to a high-ranking apparatchik."

As Tom's bags were taken inside the house, he looked at a sizeable villa probably built in the 1920s, with a wide veranda and, judging by the sounds, there was a swimming pool somewhere. "Other guests are staying here. Get changed and come and join us by the pool," said Toddy.

Tom was led upstairs to the first floor where he was shown into a large room with full-length windows that overlooked the sea. His bag looked rather small on the sizeable side table. Everything about the house was on a grand scale. No wonder the peoples' party seized it for one of their commissars, thought Tom.

Changing quickly into something more appropriate for an afternoon by the pool, Tom went back downstairs and followed the sound of the noise to where the pool was. He saw about ten people, some in the pool and others on loungers.

"Meester Scoobey?" A female voice called him over to a poolside bar. The owner of the voice had a very tanned body and very blonde hair, all wrapped in a one-piece swimsuit. The mirror sunglasses hid her eyes, but the dazzling white smile seemed genuine. She waved a hand over an array of bottles.

"Piva?" said Tom, pointing helpfully at a beer bottle.

"Of course!" she said passing over a bottle and a glass. "My name ees Tanya" she continued as Tom poured himself a drink. "You speak Russian?" she smiled. Tom said that his Russian was limited. "Too bad!" she said.

"Ah! Tom" Toddy's voice carried across the terrace as he came across the tiles to where he was standing. "I'll do some introductions later. You've met Tanya?" Toddy was wearing the same shorts and a Hawaiian shirt, which had made Tom pull a face when they met at the airport.

"Some more people are coming over this evening," said Toddy. "I just took a call from one of my associates. Gonna be quite a parteee!" He smiled at his bad American impersonation. He motioned for Tom to follow him. They walked across the wide terrace to what looked like an office. Passing through the sliding glass door, it took a moment for Tom's eyes to adjust to the different light level.

"My den!" said Toddy waving towards a large room. Tom could see all the things needed for a home office, a desktop PC, a printer, a telephone with lots of buttons for extensions, a fax machine and shelves and filing cabinets. On the wall were what looked like architectural drawings.

"My great project" explained Toddy. "A hotel resort complex". Tom tried to make sense of the drawings. Toddy waved his hand across the paper. "Main building with the hotel, sauna, gym, pool and casino" he said. Ah! thought Tom, might be worth looking a bit closer at this.

"Looks interesting..." Tom began. "Have a prospectus" said Toddy reaching for a glossy brochure. As he flicked through the pages full of idealised sketches and plans, Toddy got into sales mode. Tom largely blanked this out. What caught his attention was a list of investors, included to draw in those who wanted to buy into the scheme. The list looked impressive enough, but Tom almost exclaimed as he saw one of the investors, Falcon Holdings (Kyrenia) Ltd. Falcon Holdings was one of the companies that formed part of Lord Markham's empire.

"Very interesting" said Tom trying to keep a poker face. Toddy followed his gaze. "You'll meet some of these folks later" he said smiling at Tom. "Some of our countrymen, I mean Brits, are investing here."

Tom smiled back. His mind was racing. Before he met any of his fellow-countrymen he would need to ask Georgina and her network of elves to see what they could uncover about Falcon Holdings (Kyrenia) Ltd.

* * *

As preparations for the evening party got underway, Tom went back to his room. Varna was two hours ahead of the UK, making it mid-afternoon. He sent Georgina a text, asking her to call him as soon as possible.

A thought struck him: was the room bugged? Was this in fact an elaborate set-up by a hostile state, designed to entrap a British Member of Parliament? All he could do was carry out a quick visual check, as he had no technical support. If his bags had already been searched there would have been nothing to give the true purpose of his visit away, so he could at least relax on that score.

The electrical fittings looked antique, showing no signs of recent 'fixing'. Tom made a mental note not to touch anything electrical after he got out of the bathroom. Reassured he was more relaxed when his phone rang a few moments later.

"Sounds like you're somewhere else" said Georgina, her voice sounding suitably cautious. Tom couldn't reveal the reason for his visit so he dissembled. "Visiting an old school mate in Bulgaria" he said breezily. "Lovely place by the sea" - all of which was true.

"I just wonder if you could do a check on a company; I'm concerned my friend might be getting into bed with the wrong sorts". Tom knew that Georgina was savvy enough to see through the bluff, but he didn't want to get into a lengthy explanation over an open phone line. He explained that the party was starting in about two hours, which he hoped would give her enough time to unearth anything he needed to know.

When he told her the name of the company she understood straight away. It was she and her bunch of researchers who had unravelled Markham's network of influence. "Understood" she said. Tom knew that she had got the message.

"I'll get back to you as soon as I can" she said. I hope so, thought Tom.

8

"You'll find that Toddy is very amenable" said Darren, as their car drove along the coast road out of Varna. "You mean he's a mug?" echoed Donald smiling.

"He grew up in Britain but his family are Bulgarian" continued Darren. "He came back here after 1989 to reclaim his family property. Did quite well for himself in the property market in the UK. Didn't get hit too badly by the financial crash, so he's quids in."

"And he wants to buy his way into our little venture?" asked Donald. "Let's see the colour of his money!"

"He's sitting on some prime real estate for the project we're planning. Got some fellow Bulgars interested too – dodgy bloke called Boyko, a well-known face hereabouts..." said Darren. The car pulled off the highway along the driveway and into the open space where other cars had parked. Another group was just getting out of an expensive-looking limousine.

"So far, so good!" said Donald as a young hostess came towards them smiling. "Thees way pleez!" Darren gave Donald a nudge with his elbow: "I saw her first!"

They walked across the car parking area and through a

hedge of greenery into the poolside area where the party was already under way. They both noticed some people in the pool. "Didn't realize it was that kind of party" murmured Donald.

The hostess led them up to where Toddy was busy greeting his guests. "Ah! Darren, so good to see you again." He shook Darren's hand earnestly and gave him what seemed to Donald like a genuine smile. Darren introduced Toddy to Donald. He was given a firm handshake accompanied by the touch on the arm that politicians affected to symbolise a special connection.

"I hope we can do business together, Mr Johnson" Toddy gushed. "Let's talk a bit later but please do make yourselves at home" he said, waving towards a buffet and drinks bar. "Very kind" replied Donald, who led Darren towards the buffet.

As they walked away, Donald pulled a face. "What's that mean?" asked Darren. It was he who had brokered the meeting, as he felt Toddy would be a useful local connection. "Hmm – let's wait and see. Seems a bit too keen for my liking."

"He does gush a bit" agreed Darren "but he's *connected!*"

"As long as he's connected to the *right* people....." replied Donald.

* * *

In his room Tom re-read a briefing note that he had obtained from Oxford Info about the overall situation in Bulgaria. He could hear that the party was under way. Before his election, he had been a partner in the company which provided geopolitical advice to corporate clients. Now he was an elected MP he had chosen to be a sleeping partner to avoid any conflict of interest.

"I think I'm going to have to update this" he said to himself. The report was six months old but it might as well have been six years. Things changed fast in this part of the world, thought

Tom. He'd have to feed some local colour into his colleagues to ensure a more 'fresh' feel to their reports about the country.

There was a knock on the door. Tom put the briefing note back into his bag and walked over to the door. "Meester Scoobey?" It was Tanya, who was dressed in a very short party dress. "Pleez join Toddy in his office when you can" she said with a wide smile. "I'll be right there" he said with his best professional smile.

"Shall I wait?" she said leaning on the door frame, her smile getting wider. Tom was beginning to sense a honey trap, which he would suggest to Toddy was not appreciated. "I'll go now – shall we?" He gestured for them both to walk down to Toddy's den. He saw Tanya's eyes harden, but her smile remained. "Pleez" she said, as she led him downstairs.

They went down what had been the servants' stairs in a former era, then around the side of the house out of sight of the throng by the pool. At the door to Toddy's den she waved towards the door and turned away with a coquettish glance at him.

"Tom?" Toddy came out to greet him. "Seems like the party is going well," said Tom. He could see out through Toddy's den to where more people were in the pool and yet more were arriving.

"It's how business is done here" Toddy said, as he waved Tom inside. "A toast!" he said, as he pulled a bottle of champagne out of an ice bucket and poured them both a glass. "Old friends!" he said, as he clinked his glass with Tom's. Tom smiled and took a sip. Although they were in the same year at school, Toddy had hung out with another crowd.

"Tell me, Tom" said Toddy as he waved his guest to a plump seat, "how is it going in Parliament?" Where to begin, thought Tom; but this might be the chance to open some doors into what Toddy was up to.

"It's full on!" he said. "I'm in Westminster from Monday until Wednesday evening or Thursday. The weekend is spent in the constituency and we have Sunday to ourselves." Toddy asked him questions about whether MPs were immune from prosecution, and whether they could have interests outside of their parliamentary work. As Toddy topped up his champagne glass, Tom discerned a pattern to his questioning.

"Most MPs go into politics to make a difference: to do something for their communities, or the causes they care about," said Tom.

"I think I'd like to get into politics here, Tom, perhaps you can advise me?" Toddy's smile was genuine, maybe he really did want to give something back to the land of his fathers. Tom nodded as if to show he was thinking about it.

"You need to think about which party here is closest to your interests," said Tom.

"*This* is my interest" said Toddy waving at the collective crowd outside. "They are my people, my family and my business associates." Tom recalled Matt's comment about the Balkan code of obligation. If he was elected, he would be expected to look after his own people first.

"In Britain, you don't seem to have the same sort of relationship as we do here, with our own homeland" Toddy continued.

"Like the German heimat"? asked Tom. Toddy nodded as he took a sip of his champagne.

"My ancestors are buried here. This is *our* land! When the so-called peasants threw my family out of this place we had nothing." Tom saw Toddy's face flush with anger.

"Do you know what that means, Tom? When you have nothing, all you have left is your family and your honour." Toddy went on to explain how he had set himself the goal of regaining his family home once the post-communist regime had opened up the possibility of restitution of confiscated property.

"But in this country, you have to do deals with people, maybe people who are not so good" Toddy added. What he described was a sort of Faustian pact with some of the local communist officials who had become entrepreneurs. He had suggested that his land holdings were a good opportunity for development, and once he was elected to Parliament he could ensure that he protected his friends.

Tom hoped that his expression did not betray his dismay. Toddy was hoping to exploit his position in much the same way that Lord Markham had sought to use his preferred candidate in the safe seat of Ridgeway. Toddy seemed unaware of Tom's line of thinking, as he went over to his desk and opened one of the top drawers.

"You were a soldier, Tom" he said as he pulled an automatic pistol out of the drawer. "Did you ever see one of these?" he said, waving it around like a toy. Tom instinctively flinched as the gun barrel went past his nose.

"May I see?" he asked in what he hoped was a matey way.

He took the pistol in his right hand, and felt for the safety catch which to his relief was in the safe position. "Makarov PM" said Tom. He had been on the wrong end of one once in a bar in Mostar, when he and Sid had run into the local militia on pay day. Sid had managed to thump the offending militiaman, who felt no pain even as he slumped to the floor. But that was a story for another day.

"Very neat" added Toddy. "Always good to have some protection these days." Tom handed the gun back to Toddy who dropped it into his drawer and closed it. Not great security, thought Tom. "Do you need protection?" he asked.

"It's a way to ensure respect" Toddy replied, filling up their glasses. "Shows you are a serious person." Again Tom nodded as if to say that he understood. "We should continue this later as I'm neglecting my guests" said Toddy, swigging his champagne.

"Let's go and meet some people." He led Tom out onto the pool-side terrace.

"You might like to meet some fellow countrymen who I hope will bring something to the party!" Toddy was pleased with his play on words. He led them through the throng of people, many of whom were now in the pool. It reminded Tom of a scene from the film version of *The Great Gatsby* set in the roaring twenties.

As Toddy led him through the crowd, Tom could hear voices speaking English. A familiar tone caught his attention. In the group they headed towards, he recognised the unmistakable outline of Donald Johnson, even though he had his back turned.

"Hi guys!" gushed Toddy. "Meet my old school pal." They turned towards him with blank expressions, except for Donald, whose jaw dropped as his eyes widened in amazement.

"Small world, Don!" said Tom.

9

"How are you feeling?" Janine was the practice manager at the health centre where Anna was a GP. They were sitting in a local pub after work, at the end of the working week.

Anna made a face. "They say you should listen to your body...." she began. "The past few months have been a bit of a roller-coaster ride and it's saying – whoa!"

Janine nodded her understanding. She had been in this same pub when Anna burst in hysterical after an attempted acid attack on her. She wanted to be reassuring to her colleague and friend.

"You're going through a lot of changes" she began. She was looking deep into Anna's eyes. What she saw made her worried. "You're a tough kid, you'll get through this and you'll both have a beautiful baby."

"I know" sighed Anna "but it's been tough, can't deny it". Janine was nursing a large glass of red, to celebrate the end of the week. Anna had a glass of sparkling elderflower.

"This time last year...." began Janine.

Anna smiled. "Every New Year's Eve, Tom and I raise a glass and toast. He says 'This time last year', and I reply 'This time next year'. It sort of reminds us both of how lucky we were to find each other, given all our previous adventures."

Janine felt better seeing Anna smile. She knew that these waves of feeling low tended to wash over her since she became pregnant but soon passed. "When will Tom get back?" she asked.

"Tomorrow evening." Anna looked at her watch "It's two hours ahead in Bulgaria so he's at some schmoozy reception." She just stopped herself; people weren't supposed to know the detail of Tom's latest escapade.

"I didn't realise that being an MP's wife would be so lonely" she added. "I miss having him around the house, and then when he's back it's all systems go."

"You'll have plenty to keep you busy once mini-Scobie arrives!" said Janine trying to raise Anna's spirits. She was rewarded by a wide smile. "That's my girl!"

"I'd really like some wine but I know it's not allowed...." Anna saw Janine waving a scolding finger at her.

"You'll just have to take up knitting then!" she said. Anna laughed.

Janine noticed Anna's eyes flick, something she had previously seen in the health centre when something wasn't quite right. Anna had a sort of sixth sense, Janine reminded herself. She raised her eyebrows, to signify her understanding.

"That couple over by the big green planty thing" Anna began. "Like they're trying to hide" she added.

Janine did her best to glance unobtrusively in their direction. A man and woman were seated at a small table by the window not quite hidden from the bar, but visible from where the two friends sat. Their demeanour was tense, the woman was quite a bit younger than the man who looked a bit rough.

"Something not quite right..." Anna quickly got up as the

man left the table, passing her on his way to the toilet at the back of the room.

"Hi! I'm a medical doctor." She slid into his seat and looked straight at the girl, with her big smile. "I can't help feeling you look a bit peaky, everything OK?"

The girl looked around her nervously, as if she was afraid to speak. "I'm OK" was all she could say. Anna sensed there was something she couldn't speak about. She pushed one of her visiting cards over the table towards her, which the girl swiftly pocketed.

"Call me if you need to" she said, standing up as the man reappeared. "Can I help you, miss?" His voice was a mixture of sarcasm and menace.

"Girl talk!" said Anna, with her big smile. She had a good look at him; perhaps Tom knew who this character was. She walked back over to where Janine was sitting.

"Nasty piece of work" said Janine, as Anna sat back down. "He was giving you an evil look" she added.

Anna nodded. "Something wrong there, I hope she can get in touch somehow."

Tom and Toddy walked away from the group of Brits gathered at the poolside. Tom was pondering how Toddy had managed to get involved with them.

"Great guys!" Toddy was enthusiastic. Maybe the champagne was beginning to catch up on him. This is the right time to start probing, thought Tom, now that his inhibitions are reduced.

"How'd you meet them?" he asked in a by-the-way tone of voice.

"Through Darren, at the yacht club, great guy," said Toddy. "A really go-ahead kind of guy, really smart!"

"Are they looking to invest in your project?" asked Tom.

"Big time!" gushed Toddy. "You've no idea how much I want this, Tom. I will own this stretch of the coastline."

"You must have some local partners too?" Tom was trying not to lead Toddy too much, just enough to encourage him into some revelatory remarks.

"Yeah – as well as my family there are some guys my cousin knows, they're plugged into some Serbian and Russian folks".

Curiouser and curiouser, thought Tom. As they continued walking, Tom noticed that the group of Brits were walking away from the pool towards their cars.

"Tom, my family was dispossessed, lost everything. I can get back what we used to own, it'll be putting a wrong to right."

Well, thought Tom, there is a spark of decency there. Let's see if we can make it burn a little brighter. "Are you happy doing business with these folks?" he asked.

"Need to" said Toddy, almost as if he was trying to persuade himself. "But I need to ensure that I have legal protection."

Tom nodded. He'd have to see that Toddy got some water-tight advice. But where to start?

* * *

"This is really bad, I need to find out what *he's* doing here". Don's sudden change of behaviour was puzzling to Darren. Donald had not revealed the full story of his sudden arrival from Britain, so he would have to stall Darren while he came up with a plausible explanation for his reaction when he saw Tom. "Someone from a previous life" he had explained as they moved away from the party crowd.

After they had met, Tom had explained to Toddy that he and Donald were acquainted and left it at that. "That's great, Tom!" gushed Toddy.

Darren also took a sip of his champagne before he spoke. "Look, Don," he began "these people represent a very good investment opportunity. I've brought you into something big. We need Toddy as he has got the title to the land for this project. If there's anything I should know, maybe now would be a good time...?"

"We need to clarify Toddy's relationship with – *him.*" He gestured towards where Tom was standing. Donald was vehement. "He's bad news." Darren looked over at Tom. "Leave that to me, I'll have a word with some of my Bulgarian colleagues, and we'll get this sorted, don't you worry." Donald's expression changed. "I like the sound of that!"

10

"An intriguing conundrum" mused Matt, as he looked at his glass of wine.

For once they were all able to sit out in the garden of Shepherds Cottage and enjoy the summer weather. Tom was at home, during the parliamentary recess, and Mat and Lizzie were also on holiday away from parish duty.

"I did a debrief on my return from Varna," said Tom. "The question is, what comes next, if anything."

Matt's two boys were enjoying the garden and climbing trees under the watchful eye of Lizzie. An occasional squawk from one or other of the boys made them look to see that they were alright.

"They bounce well at that age," said Lizzie. "I like the idea that they'll learn what is safe and when to stop climbing."

Tom caught Anna's worried glance and gave her a smile.

"A few trips to A & E though" added Matt. "It sounds like Toddy wants to play with the big boys" he continued. "I wonder if he knows when to stop climbing?"

"What I'm worried about is whether the legal folks think

they can charge Toddy with something and bring him back for trial."

Tom saw the quizzical looks of the others.

"The Serious Fraud Office has had a series of near misses recently. I don't want to hand him over to face trial without the chance to steer him away from the dark side."

"Become a witness for the prosecution, you mean"? asked Lizzie. Tom nodded.

"Plus he needs to watch his own legal situation. I think he's rushing into this to salvage his family honour."

* * *

"What we have is a mosaic," said Georgina. "We were able to get a lot of information about the Markham network from the material Maude gave us."

Lord Charles Markham's network of influence and his dubious business contacts had been unmasked by his long-suffering personal assistant.

They were sitting in the skunk works – the anonymous building on the outskirts of Didcot, where Georgina and her team of investigative journalists worked. Despite the summer weather the blinds were drawn, as a precaution against leakage of electronic data, so they sat in the washed-out glow cast by overhead lighting.

"What we need to do now is to complete the picture, by asking the right questions of our citizen journalists around the world" she added.

Tom had told her about Toddy and she knew about his trip to Varna, but not about the interest of the security services in Toddy's possible connections with organised crime.

"Ideally we need to be able to convince Don Johnson that his stash of money is not safe" said Tom, to the room full of what

Georgina called her elves. They were a motley lot but had proved their worth by the work they had done unmasking Markham.

"If he realizes that his ill-gotten gains are no longer safe, he might be persuaded to shop his associates." He saw the elves nodding; they got it.

"Also we want to find out how Don Johnson is associated with Nikolai Todorov and whether this is a criminal link, or a legitimate business link."

"Now that we have this social media world the method has changed a bit" Georgina continued. "Somebody will know somebody who has their suspicions about somebody else."

Tom saw the sense of this. He remembered the intelligence cycle from his time in military intelligence. A question is posed, the information is gathered and assessed, and the question is posed again, in the light of the new information. And so on, and so on.

"How long might this process take?" asked Tom.

"More quickly than using the old methods" she replied. "There'll be false leads and dead ends; but the more we ask, the further along the road we'll get."

She saw Tom nodding.

"You go on your holidays, Tom, and we'll get on with the job."

With a friendly wave to the elves, Tom got up and walked with Georgina towards the door.

"How's Anna?" she asked.

"She's looking forward to a change of scene" Tom said with a smile. "A couple of weeks up in the Highlands, a chance to see some of her family" he added.

"Bring me back some haggis!" said Georgina with a smile.

Tom walked out into the sunlight to where his brother Mike was waiting, leaning against Molly his Land Rover.

"Seen a dodgy-looking bloke cruising around here, passed by a couple of times" said Mike, as they got into Molly. Tom made a note to let Georgina know that someone had been snooping around.

Best keep an eye out, thought Tom. It could be media interest or it could be something else.

11

"How are you doing?" Tom and Anna were walking up a sloping path around Ben Lora, one of their favourite places just outside Connel. The warm summer air brushed their faces. He was rewarded with one of Anna's broad smiles as she held her arms out, as if to embrace the whole world.

At last, peace and quiet. Anna's complexion had responded to the open air and some local food. From the top of Ben Lora, they would be able to look over the coast and surrounding countryside. A long way from the concerns of Westminster.

"I'm glad that I had that swim earlier, really woke me up" she said.

"I've never understood the compulsion to swim in a freezing cold sea!" replied Tom. "Besides, should you be swimming in your condition?"

"Sure I should!" she laughed. "You're just not a water baby like me!"

He looked at her, a mop of red hair blowing in the breeze and a big smile. Now that she was beginning to look pregnant Anna had taken to wearing loose clothes, which mostly consisted of Tom's old shirts and jumpers.

They walked back to the cabin they had rented by the side of Loch Etive. Just in time, thought Tom, as he looked up at the clouds gathering.

He had left his phone in the cabin and noticed that the light was blinking. It was a missed call from Georgina – and a voicemail.

Brad was one of the partners at Oxford Info. A Rhodes Scholar from New York State, he was one of the founders of the company. His voice was terse: "The share price has collapsed – looks like someone has dumped our stock. We're handling it from here."

* * *

This has all the hallmarks of Markham's modus operandi. Even while he was in custody he was able to get his proxies to reach out and rattle the windows. If so Tom would have to face the fact that this attack was aimed at him. It would make him very unpopular with his colleagues when they made the connection.

Something big was clearly up. He felt calm, realizing that he was in the eye of the storm but others were being buffeted. He recalled the words of one of his army instructors: 'Stay cool and solve the problem'.

When he got through to Georgina, she was able to enlighten him. "He's taken a big position in your company since you floated and has just dumped the shares" she continued.

"I'm just getting that news now" he replied. "My colleagues are firefighting."

"Look at the shareholders' register and you'll see Peregrine Nominees, that's one of Markham's investment vehicles" she continued. Tom was scribbling notes into a small book that he always kept to hand.

"What size of shareholding?"

"It's about 10 percent of your shareholders" was her short reply.

Tom tried to compute the amount but couldn't get the figure into his head. A 10% holding would represent a significant chunk of the funds they had raised through the initial share offering. Maybe that was why they had done so well?

He realized that he must get this information to the folks in London, so at least they knew what they were dealing with. This was going to be awkward to explain.

"Good luck" said Georgina and ended the call.

Tom was keying the numbers for Grant, who was the Oxford Info Finance Director. He heard his laconic Kiwi tones on voicemail suggesting that he leave a message. Tom had the feeling that he was freefalling, with nothing to grab or reach out to. He was isolated, away from the centre of things.

He would have to get back down south to be part of the solution, rather than languishing in splendid isolation on the shores of Loch Etive. His message to Grant had been received and it triggered a very terse voicemail from Brad.

"There's going to be an EGM tomorrow at ten."

No 'call me when you can' – just 'be there' was the implication.

The Directors of Oxford Info had put out a press release that the company's finances and its prospects were sound. It was obvious to Tom that there was only one thing driving investor behaviour – other than the herd mentality of nervous speculators - and that was the presence of T. Scobie as one of the management.

He managed to get through to Muriel, at home in the constituency. "How're you doing?" she asked gently.

"Managing" was the best he could think of.

"It's all over the local news, even a bit on the national news" she added.

"Must be a slow news day" said Tom, aware that he was in danger of becoming the story.

This could wreck everything he and others had done over the past few years, to build Oxford Info up to its present position.

"The Party Leader's office has been in touch" she began, in a foreboding tone. "They want clarity on where you stand in all of this business about Oxford Info. They're unaware of your connection to the company".

Just what a media-conscious Party Leader doesn't want. Especially when you've run your campaign on a platform of being a new broom, come to clean out the stables. Not good for the image.

"I'm one of the partners of the company. We've listed on the AIM and there has been some speculation about the company, which has been playing out during the day." Tom heard himself repeating the language of the Oxford Info media comment.

"The Party Leader wants this to go away in the next 24 hours" Muriel said neutrally – just passing on the message you understand, was the tone of her voice.

Stay cool and solve the problem, Tom remembered.

"It'll be solved in 24 hours, don't you worry." Tom sounded more confident than he felt. The next call did nothing to improve his mood. It was Grant.

"Peregrine Nominees have filed a petition to wind up the company. What's going on, Tom?"

"Sounds like a co-ordinated effort to discredit us."

"We can delay the process with our legal folks, but I'm not sure what we can do about the share price." Grant's laconic voice had an edge to it.

"I'll have to get down for the EGM, but let's stay in touch. We'll think of something. We didn't come this far to be thwarted by some clown who is playing out a personal grudge." Tom tried to inject some steel into his voice.

"Hope you're right, Tom" was all Grant could say.

That's all we can do, thought Tom - hope.

12

"The dark night of the soul, Tom." Matt's voice sounded stern, even if his intention was kindly.

As Anna had driven him to Glasgow Central to catch the first available train, Tom had been on the phone. The arrangements for the EGM were being thrown together by lawyers, financial PR people and colleagues at Oxford Info. Several of his colleagues had called him to say that as he was the cause of the run on the company's share price, he ought to consider his position. He felt like the Ancient Mariner. He had always seen Oxford Info as a tightly knit group of colleagues. This had driven a wedge between them.

Tom needed to talk things through with someone and Anna had suggested he called Matt. A call from his cousin was a welcome interruption for Matt, who was working on the report for his annual Parochial Church Meeting.

"You have come so far, Tom." Matt's familiar tones on the phone drilled through the fog of self-pity which had enveloped him.

"I just feel so weary" Tom heard himself say.

"Are you beaten?"

Tom heard the reproach in Matt's voice. It reminded him of an instructor at a low point during his officer training course: '*D'you want to jack it in, sir?*' – not then, and not now.

"I think our friend might have overplayed his hand," said Tom.

The thought came out of nowhere. What did that mean? he asked himself.

"You will have to convince the EGM of that" replied Matt.

"If I'm the cause of this problem, then I will have to lay the facts before the EGM. Investors can be as skittish as horses at the start of a big race, but once they get going they like to win."

Tom let the thought hang in the air. He wanted to see how Matt responded. He had more experience of the corporate world, so he should be able to judge how a sceptical audience would respond. His response was equivocal.

"You'll have to fly by the seat of your pants on this, Tom."

Tom remembered the aviator's wisecrack that any landing you walked away from was a good one, so he took Matt's advice. They ended the call with Matt saying that he would be thinking of him tomorrow.

* * *

He managed to arrive late in the evening at the hotel where the EGM would be held next day. Tom slept fitfully and got an extra early start to his day when his phone rang in the small hours. Through the fuzziness, he heard Will Gibney's stentorian tones.

"What'n hell is goin' on with that company of yours, Tommy?"

Will was another Rhodes Scholar who knew Brad, and who had put some money into Oxford Info in the early days, before Tom joined the team.

"A bad guy is trying to sink the company" Tom said as he got out of bed and walked around the bedroom.

"Nothin' else? No black holes?" Will's voice was anxious.

"No, we are – were fully capitalized. Our business plan has been fully audited. This is about the person who was the puppeteer behind my principal rival for the candidacy for the Ridgeway seat".

"Sounds like a bad guy alright." Will sounded reassured.

"Tell you what, lemme make some calls" he said. "No promises, mind" and he rang off.

Tom looked at his phone. Had Will just thrown him, and Oxford Info, a lifeline? Maybe it was already too late.

* * *

Tom and his colleagues gathered in the soulless conference room which the company had hired in a hotel on the outskirts of Oxford. They were talked through the chronology of events by one of the bankers involved in the floatation. Tom felt compelled to speak to his co-workers before the atmosphere became too unpleasant.

"Like many of you, I was astonished to hear what has happened." He saw a group of sceptical faces who he felt were listening out of politeness. He would need to be convincing.

"Since I got involved in the candidacy for the Ridgeway seat, a local personality sought to frustrate me. This has included arranging a car accident that nearly killed my brother, and an attack on my wife."

"So where does this leave us?" asked a voice from among the group.

"It still leaves us short of funding" replied the banker matter-of-factly.

"It means that the petition to wind up the company can be

contested, and we can prove that we are a going concern" came another voice.

"That's the crocodile closest to the canoe" said Brad ruminating, as if he was beginning to see a way out of this dilemma.

"How do we present this information to the investors?" asked Jürgen, another of the founding partners. Always the practical German, he was looking for a workable solution.

"We start with the fundamentals" responded Brad, rallying.

"We have a good proposition which meets customers' needs" he continued. "We need to reassure investors that the fundamentals are sound."

Tom could see one of the bankers looking at his watch; it was nearly time for the meeting to start. A group was milling in the hallway outside the conference room.

"I'm just going to step out and see if I can identify any particular faces" he said. He had a feeling that Markham would have arranged for one of his stooges, possibly one of the Bandits, to report on how matters unfolded. The Bandits were a list of people identified by a former chairman of the constituency association as Markham's willing tools. He found his way through the group to a coffee pot placed on a table and helped himself to a cup. As he wandered among them, he scanned their faces.

There – one of the Bandits. A solicitor called Neil something, who was on a list given to him by Henry Makepeace during the election campaign. Tom had seen him at one of Markham's social events at Wyvern Hall. He kept looking to see if there were any others he recognised. As he continued, a figure came out of the crowd. It was Georgina.

"Morning, Tom. Got to stop meeting like this!" Her manner was breezy and lifted Tom's spirits. Here was a potential ally.

"Do you have something to reassure the mob?" she asked. He could hear the anticipation in her voice.

"Enough" Tom began. "It all depends on that article" he said, nodding towards the figure of Neil who was studiously buried in a newspaper.

She recognized the quotation from the Duke of Wellington on the eve of Waterloo.

"I hope you can hold out long enough for the cavalry to arrive" she said gravely.

"So do I." He gave her what he hoped was a winning smile, but his heart wasn't in it.

"Let's speak once the proceedings are concluded" he added, "I'd better get back to my colleagues."

With that he re-entered the meeting room. As he did so, he was conscious that there was still an atmosphere of muted hostility. Their situation was the result of some petulant ego fight between Tom and some local character who had the wherewithal to play the markets, and they felt like pawns.

"We've got some speakerphones set up for a conference call to relay the proceedings" said the banker.

Good, thought Tom, that'll give us a wider audience.

"What about the press?" asked one of the financial PR people.

"We have nothing to hide." Tom jumped in before any dissenting voices could speak.

Brad shot him a hostile glance.

"You and your 'Mr. Smith goes to Washington' antics have got us into this mess, Tom!" he barked.

The room fell silent.

"We have just been talking about how sound the fundamentals are, Brad, we have nothing to fear from the media reporting that fact."

Tom met Brad's glare.

"Tom is right, Brad", Jürgen's voice was sweet reason.

Brad nodded silently, still holding Tom's gaze. This isn't over, he seemed to imply.

"I suggest we stick to the agenda, folks" said the financial PR person, brightly. "That's what we have circulated to investors – and to media" he added.

"United we stand, divided we fall," said Jürgen.

13

The atmosphere in the meeting room was not propitious. The strip lighting washed everyone in a pale light. Tom, Brad and the others walked through the room, up onto the staging set at one end. The conference speakerphones crackled, adding to the sense of an impending storm. The crowd of investors and a few reporters settled themselves into their seats. One of the financial PR people introduced one of the bankers who began to speak. As he did so Tom kept his eyes on Neil, seated at the back of the room. He was watching for any sign of his mood. Doubtless Markham had given him instructions, but how did he feel about them now that he was in the room?

"When are we going to get some answers?" called an angry voice from the back of the room. The banker was flustered by the interruption.

"Ladies and Gentlemen" Brad began. "We stand one hundred percent behind the prospectus we originally laid before you."

His New York tones reminded Tom of the speeches of President Kennedy. Still no move from Neil. As Brad continued to speak, Tom caught sight of Neil shifting his glance to another member of the audience, a co-conspirator. He was orchestrating the objectors, who would throw out queries and either drag out the proceedings or spook the others. The journalists were watching. He had to be headed off.

Tom stood up, causing Brad to turn his head while he continued speaking.

"When are *we* going to get some answers, Neil?"

Tom had used his best parade-ground voice, so that there was no chance of anybody in the room, or listening on the conference call, not hearing.

"Tell us why we are here, Neil!"

The financial PR person stood up as if to calm down the meeting. Tom gave him a look: Not Now. He sat down again. Brad looked at Jürgen, and then back at Tom. It was now or never.

"Ladies and Gentlemen" Tom began in a more measured voice, but with his gaze fixed firmly on Neil; nowhere to run, my boy.

"There is only one false prospectus that need concern us today. It is that proposed by Peregrine Holdings of whom Mr Neil Fowler is a representative."

Tom held out his arm to show the rest of the room where Neil was sitting. His face was ashen but immobile.

"Peregrine bought a block of shares, which helped to ramp up the price of the issue. So, either something fundamental has changed, or they were being fraudulent."

Tom let the thought sink in. The room was silent.

"So, which is it?" came a voice from the middle of the room.

"I think the gentleman might give us an answer!" Brad's voice cut through the atmosphere.

There was a collective murmuring in the audience. Neil was

busy shuffling papers on his knee. The banker and the financial PR person looked at each other; they wanted to regain control of the meeting. Tom caught the eye of the banker.

"I think the meeting should hear from the representative of Peregrine Holdings" he said to the room in general.

The banker looked at his agenda momentarily, considering whether this might shorten proceedings. He looked at Neil.

"Do you wish to contribute, Mr Fowler?" His tone was neutral.

Neil remained in his seat. Whatever stratagem he and his co-conspirators had agreed, this was not the plan. Did he have a plan B?

"Shall we vote on the petition to wind up the company?" asked Tom, seeking to flush out Neil's accomplices.

"What a lot of nonsense!" said an irritated voice from the back of the room. "Waste of all our time!"

"Those in favour of a winding up order?" continued Tom.

Neil raised his arm. He was alone.

Honour among thieves, thought Tom.

"Those against?" A forest of arms was raised.

"The petition is defeated" interjected the banker, sensing that the mood of the room was changing.

There was a smattering of applause from the gathering.

"Ladies and Gentlemen"- the banker sought to regain some control of the meeting. "We should now move onto the prospects for the company. Do we agree that Oxford Info constitutes a going concern?"

If the investors still had faith in the prospectus, there was hope that the financing package could be re-structured.

"Agreed!" several voices rang out. At which point one of the speakerphones, which had remained silent, burst into life.

"Good morning, everybody", came a voice with the twang of

the southern states of the USA. It was the voice of Will Gibney. "I have the honour to represent Carolina Investments. We're a VC fund."

There was a buzz in the room; if a Venture Capital fund was listening in, investors could get their positions secured.

"We stand ready to buy the shares dumped by Peregrine Holdings." The disembodied voice oozed contempt for the short sellers.

Tom's gaze went back to where Neill was sitting. He was leaning forward talking to another figure in a pin- striped three-piece suit, whom Tom didn't recognize. They both glanced in his direction.

"Does Peregrine Holdings accept the offer?" asked the banker.

A nod. They were beaten.

The room broke out in communal applause at no-one in particular, breaking the tension. Their collective investments were saved and the company's future secured.

Tom slumped back in his chair whilst the banker went through some formalities to record the proceedings and declare the meeting closed. Tom saw Georgina make a beeline for Neil, with a recorder which she proffered him. He pushed it away and elbowed past her, with no comment. She caught Tom's eye and gave him a broad grin. She indicated that she had to file her story and hurried out of the room.

Tom felt a clap on his back; it was Brad standing over him, his hand extended.

"Put it there, brother!" he grinned. "Never let me play poker with you, Tom!" he added as Tom stood up to shake hands.

For once Jürgen let his guard down.

"*Wunderbar*!!" he exclaimed as he embraced Tom.

"I say, steady on, old chap!" Tom responded, in his best

Bertie Wooster voice, as he disentangled himself from the bear-hug.

"Damn, we really whopped their asses!" said Brad, playing along with the spirit of national stereotypes.

I certainly hope so, thought Tom.

14

"Talk about dodging a bullet!" said Georgina. They were sitting in the kitchen of Shepherds Cottage, nursing a glass of wine. It was the day after the EGM.

"Well, we dodged it" Tom replied. "Let's hope that I can see the next one coming..."

Georgina didn't quite know how to respond. Was Tom expecting another bullet, whether real or metaphorical? So she changed the subject. "What is it that makes a man like Markham go so bad, do you suppose?"

"No obvious reason" mused Tom. "You'd have to ask Anna. She has a very good feel for people, what I think the shrinks call emotional intelligence. Perhaps we should ask her."

As if on cue Anna walked into the room. Georgina noticed how pale she looked compared to how she remembered her; perhaps the pregnancy was having an effect on her. Anna agreed to come south once Tom got on the train. She was wearing one of Tom's rugby shirts and jeans.

"Hi, Georgie!" The smile was still the same. Anna slid beside Tom, onto the bench seat against the wall. Tom got up to pour her a glass of her cordial which he passed over to her as he sat back down.

"We were just examining Markham's motivation" began Georgina. "What makes him so bent on revenge on Tom in particular?"

"Goodness! There's a question" Anna replied, taking a sip from her glass. "I've been doing some reading about criminal psychology since we began encountering his lordship and his cronies." From Tom's reaction Georgina could see that this was news to him.

"Most of what we do as GPs is a bit of applied psychology" she continued. "Might have a change of direction, once mini-Scobie makes an appearance" she added, tapping her bump. She turned towards Tom and gave him that winning smile, as if to say, Any questions?

"Lots to unpack about motivation and who was an early influence on his life" she began.

"He's an only child" Georgina replied. "Over-achiever at school". Tom saw Anna nodding as she absorbed the information.

"Plus the lure of money" added Georgina. "He probably worked out that he was smarter than most of the people around him, and he obviously enjoyed having power over people."

Tom was not surprised to hear this, it seemed to be something he had understood without knowing why. Most of the bad guys in the Balkans were thugs with guns making money, and he had seen a slightly different version of this at Toddy's party. Markham was content to be the puppet master getting people to do his bidding, whatever their motivation might be.

"He's still at it, from behind bars," said Georgina. "You can say that again" echoed Tom. "That little episode with Oxford Info was a way of letting us know that he hasn't gone away."

"That's his weakness," said Anna. "He thinks that the rules of nature don't apply to him, so he makes mistakes. After all, that's why he's in prison."

Tom couldn't help smiling as he heard Anna diagnosing Markham as if she were discussing a patient in a clinic. After all she had been through as a result of Markham's scheming over the vacancy for the Ridgeway seat, she had emerged much stronger, almost fierce. Perhaps it was her maternal instinct asserting itself, as she sought to protect their unborn child from the likes of Markham and co.

"Markham made a big mistake when he overplayed his hand with the choice of candidate for Ridgeway" said Tom. "He came up against a bunch of honest folk who weren't going to stand for it."

Tom saw Georgina nodding silently. She caught his eye and he saw that she was blinking away tears in remembrance of her colleague Jack, who did not survive his encounter with Markham and his cronies.

"That girl you saw in the pub" Georgina began, looking at Anna. "Might she be a pawn in one of Markham's little schemes?" Anna had spoken to Tom after the episode with the odd-looking couple she had seen. Something wasn't right she had thought. Her description seemed to fit one of the Pascoe boys, as bad as the Smurfits, Tom had said. But there would need to be more proof.

"Possibly, but I've heard nothing," said Anna.

"Easier to move people than drugs," said Georgina. "Easy to forge papers from some countries" she added.

Not for the first time Tom found himself not quite believing the kind of conversation they were having around their table in Shepherds Cottage.

* * *

"We need to think this through, Don" said Darren with an urgent tone in his voice. "We're onto a goldmine here, so we need to think about whether we're serious, or just playing at this." His tone was anything but friendly.

They had returned to Northern Cyprus from Varna and gone their separate ways for a couple of days to deal with everyday matters. Agreeing to meet to sort out the Varna opportunity, they were in a beachside tavern, where they felt safe to speak.

Don had been knocked back by the sight of Tom Scobie at the event in Varna. He knew that he needed to maintain Markham's business interests, and where possible to augment them like a good steward, through cultivating new opportunities. The attempt to dump the shares of Oxford Info had been thwarted by Scobie being able to rally support, but his luck had to run out one day.

"I think we need a bit more due diligence on this chap Toddy" said Don. "He could be the weak link in this whole enterprise, despite his property holdings." He was referring to the fact that Toddy owned the land on which the Varna enterprise would be developed.

"Agreed" said Darren. "I don't think the brothers like weak links. Dead men tell no tales"

Don nodded his agreement. He saw Darren smiling in acknowledgement. They ordered some more drinks and settled down to enjoy their good fortune. As they chatted Don ran through in his mind the opportunity to remove Toddy if needed and the need to discredit Tom, removing him as a threat. It might need extreme measures, which would be tricky to organise. Well, he'd proved his ability to solve problems, so another challenge was something he looked forward to.

"There's a journalist that Scobie talks to, a right little toerag," said Don. "We had to get one out of the way during the election campaign, so I suppose it won't be too hard to do the same again" he added. "People don't think that lightning strikes twice....."

"I'll leave that up to you," said Darren. "I'm more concerned about the local situation; my Russian friends are serious." He leaned closer to Donald "if they think Toddy can be bought, they'll buy him. If they think he's a danger, they'll get rid of him."

Don made a face: "If you can't stand the heat..." He took a swig of his drink.

As he did so, he took the opportunity to have a good look at the person sitting opposite him. They were comparatively new acquaintances, and he recalled something Markham had said to him: 'Always try before you buy"; and he hadn't had the chance to test how reliable this fellow was. Maybe he needed to contrive a test of his own, before he got too far into bed with this lot.

15

Anna hated Mondays. Now that Parliament had returned after the summer recess, Tom was away until Wednesday evening in Westminster, so she faced two empty evenings until he returned. She had rediscovered many of her extended family who wanted to come and visit after the fuss surrounding the election. It was great to catch up, even if it was hard work entertaining on her own. This week she had drawn a blank; so it was going to be a couple of nights in front of the telly.

"Nights are drawing in" said one of her colleagues as they packed up for the evening. Anna made a face. Another year on its way out, but at least mini-Scobie seemed to have settled down and she felt more like herself. Something to look forward to.

She reached into her desk drawer and picked up her phone, which was switched off during her consultations. She scrolled through the text messages. There was one from Tom wishing her a good day and he'd call when he could. Others were from friends and relatives. She noticed a missed call about 30 minutes beforehand. A number she didn't recognise; maybe they'll call back.

She busied herself with the paperwork after the afternoon session of consultations, requests for lab tests and some test results to read. May as well plough through this lot, she thought. As if on cue her phone rang. She saw it was from the same number.

"Doctor Anna?" The voice sounded like the girl in the pub and she sounded anxious. Anna's mind shifted back into doctor mode.

"Hello, this is Anna, how can I help you?" She kept her voice level and calm, as if this was just another phone call. She could hear the caller gasping for breath which Anna recognised as a reaction to stress and fear.

"You said to call" continued the voice. Anna knew that she needed to calm her down, but that she might not have long to speak.

"Are you safe?" she asked.

"No – not safe, but ok to speak" came a breathy response.

"Where are you?" said Anna reaching for a notepad. She caught sight of Janine and signalled for her to come over.

"Farmyard in countryside" was the response. "I can get away - can you help me?" Before Anna could think of a response the phone call was cut short.

"Maybe it wasn't safe for her to continue" she said to herself as Janine drew up a chair. "Person at risk" said Anna. "What's the protocol when we get contacted?"

"You can text them to say they can call when it's safe to do so." Janine was all business. "Tell them to keep their phone on silent so it doesn't alert anybody when you message them." Janine watched as Anna tapped out what she hoped was a simple message.

"Should I call the police?" Anna asked.

"Maybe wait until you know a bit more" said Janine, hesitating as if she was in two minds. They agreed that it was better to call the police when they knew more. Anna reminded Janine about the encounter in the pub where they all went at the end of their working week. The dodgy man and the frail-looking girl, something not quite right about the set-up, she thought.

"Did you tell Tom?" asked Janine.

"Yes, and he passed it on to that reporter who he works with, but not the police or anything."

"I'm going to text Tom and see what he thinks about this" said Anna, as she tapped out a short 'CALL ME ASAP' to Tom. Janine was protective of Anna, after the attempted acid attack during the election campaign, so she told Anna to call her if anything came up.

Anna finished her paperwork and headed home. Driving through the familiar lanes she noticed the leaves on the trees beginning to change colour as autumn advanced. She kept her phone where she could see it but there were no calls while she drove.

The house felt like a safe haven although they'd had security lights and CCTV fitted after the arson attack during the election campaign. The lights came on as she drove into the short drive outside Shepherds Cottage to light her way to the front door.

She always enjoyed speaking to Tom while he was away, even though the separation was just a few days. The sound of his voice gave her a warm feeling that everything would be alright.

"If you get another call, get in touch with Sid. He's got a clever way of finding where mobile phones are. The trouble is that the signal on the Downs is a bit patchy. It sounds like she might be somewhere out there."

The rest of the call was about their plans for the weekend and how her pregnancy was progressing. Things had settled down after a rocky start when Anna felt miserable and sick.

"First thing I'm going to do is have a good stiff whisky" she said. "It'll help us both sleep!" Her own doctor had warned her that drinking would quickly feed into her breast milk, which Anna thought would be a good idea.

"Nice to hear you sounding chirpy" said Tom as they wrapped up the call. He didn't expect any late votes on Wednesday, so would be back in the wee hours.

* * *

"Alright Tom?" It was Kat's cheery voice that he heard as they walked into the chamber of the House of Commons. Prime Minister's questions or PMQs was a must for all MPs, as the new Prime Minister defended the coalition's programme of legislation.

The chamber of the House of Commons is smaller than people imagine. When the wartime damage was being repaired, Winston Churchill had suggested that the original dimensions be retained. The increased number of MPs, following various voting reforms, meant that the chamber took on the air of a cockpit.

"It's been a long week" replied Tom with a weary smile. Kat gave him a friendly wave as they went their separate ways.

Tom was content to sit through the session even as his colleagues were bobbing up down on the green benches, to catch the Speaker's eye and ask a question. He was going to visit a school in the constituency on Friday so he would like to relate his impressions of PMQs to the pupils who would probably be voting in the next election.

Even so his attention wandered amidst the hoo-ha. He spotted Kat on the benches opposite; like him, her attention was elsewhere as she was looking towards the press gallery. He followed her gaze and spotted one of the journalists who he recognized: Gordon the muckraker. He was looking directly at Tom.

Tom met his stare and gave him a friendly wave and a smile. He was met with a scowl, as the journalist decided to leave his place. Tom looked across the chamber to see Kat making a sign that they should speak at the end of the session. He nodded his agreement.

"That creepy bloke was giving you evils alright" said Kat as they walked out through the members' lobby. "Something I should know?"

"Search me" Tom shrugged. "I've met him once before. I'll ask one of my more media-savvy chums"

Leaving the members' lobby they walked out through the cavernous space of central lobby. The echoing noise reminded Tom of a Victorian railway station.

"After that recent episode with your old company, you've caught the attention of the press alright" continued Kat. "He picks up rumours and creates a so-called public interest story out of them" she added. "He did a number on one of my colleagues recently. He ought to have sued the cretin..."

"As long as he leaves Anna alone, I can look after myself" Tom said as they carried on walking.

"How is she?" asked Kat, happy to change the subject.

"Much better, seems to have got through the early months after a bad bout of the blues" he explained.

"She still practising, as a doctor I mean?" They continued walking towards the members' tearoom which despite its name also served lunch.

"She's trying to wangle some study leave and sort out maternity cover," said Tom. "I had no idea the NHS could be so bureaucratic! I'm expecting her to turn up at one of my constituency surgeries one of these days."

They congratulated themselves that they had missed the rush after PMQs and took their lunches to an empty table and sat down. The members' tearoom continued the theme of nondescript furnishings, reminding Tom of one of the officers' messes he had visited once upon a time.

"Wrong seat, madam! I think you'll find your *friends* over there." It was the red-faced buffoon who had accosted Tom at the reception for new members in the Speaker's house.

"The lady is my guest" said Tom, giving him a certain look. He was met with a scowl. "Be careful who your friends are, Scobie" and with that he waddled off to sit alongside one of the knights of the shires.

"Trouble with him" said Kat, drawing closer to Tom, "he's not yet managed to entrance any of the new female MPs........ We've been warned about him!"

"May I join you"? Another new MP put down his plate and sat down. He introduced himself as an MP from one of the Lake District constituencies.

"Tom, who was that goon in the press gallery staring at you?"

Tom and Kat looked at each other. Had it been so obvious that he was the object of this person's stare?

"We were wondering that" Kat replied. "Some sort of muckraking bloke" she added while Tom was eating.

"I know who he is" said Tom. "What I want to know is what his game is. Who knows the press gallery well enough to know what he's up to?"

"Er, well that one" said their companion as he looked at the red-faced MP tucking into some shepherd's pie.

"Well, that might explain something, but I don't get the feeling he is minded to be helpful" said Tom.

16

"*Vranyo*" said Tom, to no-one in particular. It was Sunday lunchtime in Shepherds Cottage. Matt and Lizzie had joined them for lunch.

"Banjo?" Lizzie was unclear what Tom was talking about. Tom could tell by the puzzled faces that his random thought had been a little bit *too* random.

"A Russian concept." Tom began trying not to sound like a schoolteacher addressing a bunch of dim pupils. "I'm lying to you, you know that I'm lying. I *know* that you know I'm lying, but I'm going to lie anyway."

"Have you learnt that since you went to the House of Commons"? asked Lizzie brightly. Tom gave her a mock scowl by way of reply.

"Well, it is something I keep in mind" he replied. "Perhaps we don't go in for barefaced lying with such bravado" he added.

"What are you thinking about?" asked Matt as Tom took a sip of wine. Tom respected Matt's insight into human nature, so was glad of the chance to explore this thought with him.

"Just trying to think my way into how someone like Toddy

who grew up here came to be in cahoots with a bunch of villains in his homeland" replied Tom.

"He needs validation" replied Matt. "He's got to be successful, so he looks for those who are successful in that society."

"And to complicate matters, there is the Markham dimension" added Anna. "What are the chances of Toddy getting hooked up with people who are involved with Markham and company?"

Tom didn't believe in coincidence, but it was just possible that the connection was made by chance. Either that, or Markham or Don Johnson had gone looking for a potential partner and Toddy came into his sights.

He shrugged. "Small world" he suggested. "I got the feeling that Don Johnson was at an early stage of talking to them, but I can't be sure."

"How can you find out, without asking Toddy?" asked Anna. "Is he coming this way anytime soon?"

Tom nodded slowly as he was chewing his food. "I'm going to have to contrive another conversation with him."

"Here or there?" asked Lizzie. She wanted to ensure that the conversation around the table did not turn into blokes bigging each other up. "You met him on his turf last time; could you invite him over here and take him for a walk in the park or something"?

"Good idea" said Tom. "I can think of all sorts of reasons to invite him over. The old school is having a fundraiser, and they have asked me to speak at their event. Might just be the right opportunity".

"Will he buy it?" asked Anna.

"It'll play to his ego" Tom replied. "I might sound him out on making a donation for the new science block, with his name on it"!

"Perfect!" said Matt.

* * *

"Oops!" said Tom as he put the phone down. He was back in his parliamentary office in Portcullis House the following afternoon.

"Problem?" said Amy leaning on the connecting door frame in the suite of offices he used. She had got to know Tom in the short time they'd been working together. He wasn't one for exaggeration, so this sounded like trouble.

"It seems that the Serious Fraud Office would like to speak to Toddy if he sets foot in this country" he said.

Tom had outlined his thoughts in a conversation with Adam from the security services, who had just called him back to give him a friendly heads-up.

"They could technically arrest him, but either way if word got back to his friends in Bulgaria, they would not be pleased" he explained.

Amy leant against the door frame and pushed her glasses up over her head. "Then you need to go to see him first" was her suggestion.

Tom nodded as he thought about the idea. Amy was wise beyond her years, so Tom had got used to bouncing ideas off her. The problem would be getting away while the Commons was sitting. The whips were against absences unless he could be paired with another absent MP from the opposition. The fewer people who knew about this the better, so he was against asking Kat for a favour just in case it leaked.

"How do I get slipped?" he asked Amy, referring to the parliamentary term for having leave of absence. Amy saw the problem and suggested that as a member of the Foreign Affairs Committee he could go and do some sort of fieldwork in Bulgaria.

They both saw that this was stretching plausibility a bit too far.

"Are you still a Reservist"? she suggested. "Have you got some days left to do this year? Didn't I see something about a big NATO exercise taking place in the Black Sea region?"

"Brilliant!" Tom clapped his hands together at the idea.

After he left the regular army Tom had agreed to stay on the Reserve list. Several of his parliamentary colleagues were also ex-military; one of them was now on a tour of duty in Afghanistan.

"I need to talk to my Reservist mates and see what's cooking."

Even so, there remained the fact that Adam was now aware of how he had been thinking. Perhaps he might have to indulge in some *Vranyo* of his own, to keep Toddy away from the clutches of the SFO.

17

"Boys on tour!" said Sid, as they drove out of Mihail Kogalniceanu airport outside Constanta in Romania. The airport was being used as a transit base for the NATO exercise. Alongside tourist flights, military transports were parked across the other side of the airfield.

"How far to the Bulgarian border?" asked Sid, as he pulled onto the motorway heading south.

"Depends on how fast you want to go" said Tom, looking at the map. "Let's not push our luck, we've got away with it so far!"

Tom had been able to talk his way into a role as a liaison officer, along with Sid as another Reservist. The whips had been accommodating thanks to a chance encounter in the voting lobby. There were no knife- edge votes due for a week or so, and Tom's voting record was good so far. A week later and they had managed to make the system work.

Tom and Sid were both in the same infantry regiment, in the reconnaissance platoon. They were both asked to join the NATO taskforce working in the Balkans after the Bosnian civil war. They knew the area from a tour of duty they'd done, and they had caught the eye of a British general involved in the peace-keeping mission.

Tom had crossed borders in this region during his time with the NATO task force looking for organised crime groups involved with smuggling weapons and other contraband. He had a good line in bluffing his way past bored customs officers.

"With any luck we'll hit the border just as they're thinking about going off shift, so we need to get a move on" he said.

And so it proved. To add to their good fortune, it had started to rain, which would make the border guards even more miserable.

"Were heading for Dobrich and then we can pick up the road to Varna," said Tom. The Land Rover rattled along as Sid kept just inside the speed limit. The last thing they needed was a stroppy traffic cop looking for a backhander.

"How's your lovely lady these days?" asked Sid. "Must be getting close now."

"She's got one of her many cousins visiting while I'm away. Some sort of therapist..... last I heard, Anna was practising breathing and doing yoga and all sorts!" replied Tom.

Tom had told Anna that he would be away for a week. She had given him a look that would curdle milk when he told her he was going on another of his 'boy scouting' trips.

"Just you keep out of trouble, Tom Scobie" she had said with the merest hint of a smile. She knew that Tom was pursuing a valiant cause, but she worried all the same.

"The good news is that I've managed to get Sid involved as my driver" he said, enfolding her in his arms. Anna liked Sid, he was like a sort of wayward brother.

"Good! He'll keep an eye on you" she said as she rested her head on his shoulder.

* * *

Anna's phone pinged. She looked at the bedside clock. 12:15 the figures glowed in the gloom. She had just dropped off to sleep. Did she dream that her phone went? She reached for the bedside light as she found her phone. A text message.

PLEASE CALL ME

It was from the girl she had seen in the pub. She sat up to collect her thoughts. Probably better to text her to see if it was safe to speak.

CAN YOU SPEAK?

She sat back and thought about what she might say, and what she could do to help. Both Tom and Sid were away, so she would have to call on Tom's brother Mike who worked on the family farm as a mechanic and handyman. He drove Tom around on constituency work and knew the problems that could arise. They had been forced off the road during the election campaign by one of Markham's goons.

Anna got out of bed and turned on the main light. She looked expectantly at her phone; another ping told her that it was safe to speak. She pressed the call button and heard a ringing tone.

"Doctor Anna?" She heard the anxious voice - barely a whisper.

"This is Anna, are you safe to talk?" She kept her voice steady and business-like, to instil some confidence in the caller.

"Is OK, but I cannot stay here. I must leave quick or they send me into a club for dancing."

Anna could picture the girl she remembered from the brief encounter in the pub. She looked young and was of small build, just the sort of thing some men liked to ogle.

"Do you know where you are?" Anna asked. "Are you in a town or in the country?"

"Is a farm with lots of old trucks. Is called Meadow Farm but is no meadow, only trucks and lots of dogs."

"Is there anybody else with you?" There might be other girls in the same position, and it could be a matter of arranging a police raid to rescue them.

As she was speaking, the door to her bedroom opened and her cousin Naomi came in, wrapping her dressing gown around her. Anna put her finger to her lips to signify the need for silence. Naomi nodded and sat at the end of Anna's bed.

"Other girls they gone tonight, is why I can call, only one man here." Anna felt a jolt of energy surge through her, somehow they had to get this girl out tonight.

"What is your name?" she said, as she felt her breath quickening. "Sonya" came the reply.

"Listen Sonya, if you can get out of the building, we will come and find you, ok?"

"Is dogs everywhere" came the reply. Anna had to think.

"Stay where you are just now and I'll call you back, OK?" Sonya reluctantly agreed.

"I promise we won't be long" she said and ended the call. She looked at Naomi who was staring at Anna with bewilderment. No time for lengthy explanations, thought Anna.

"Put some warm clothes on, we're off on a quick trip up onto the Downs" she said with a smile that signalled action.

Anna found Mike's number and called - blow the time, she thought. Mike would understand the urgency.

"Alright, Anna?" he asked, sounding as if he had just been woken in the middle of a dream.

"Does Meadow Farm ring a bell?" asked Anna.

"Ha! Yes, it's more like a junk yard. Pascoes own it, they're up to no good up there, in cahoots with the Smurfit clan" he said, sounding more awake.

Anna quickly outlined the need for a flying visit with a view to getting Sonya out.

"Give me five minutes" Mike replied. "Have you got someone there with you?" he asked. "We'll need a second pair of hands."

Anna said yes, and that her cousin was a fitness instructor which could be useful. They ended the call and Anna threw on a pair of track suit bottoms and one of Tom's sweatshirts.

"What's cooking, cuz?" asked Naomi.

"I'll tell you as we go" said Anna.

* * *

"*Buna Seara*!" said Tom as the Romanian border guard approached his side window. In the rainy gloom the guard indicated that they should show their papers.

"British Army, NATO exercise!" continued Tom, as the guard examined their identity cards. He had put on his best impression of a self-important buffoon. He pointed at the shoulder patches they had acquired on landing at the airfield, recognisable as a NATO badge. They had cost Sid a half-bottle of scotch and several packets of cigarettes from some American truck drivers.

Over the shoulder of the guard Tom could see the concrete cabin that housed the border checkpoint. Inside he could see a supervisor taking an interest in the proceedings. Tom needed to get this over with before the supervisor could intervene.

"Dobrich, Varna" he said and waved the road map under the nose of the guard, while tapping his wristwatch to indicate they were in a hurry.

"Is good!" said the border guard, giving Tom a salute. "All go home" he said pointing in the direction of the Bulgarian checkpoint. Good news, thought Tom, they'd have a clear run. He waited while the guard walked over to raise the barrier.

"*Multumesc!*" said Tom, as Sid put his foot on the accelerator, to get them moving again.

"What's our timetable?" asked Sid as they drove on into the night. They were supposed to report to the exercise controller, an American admiral who was based at Chayka naval base in Varna. A perfect opportunity to call in and see Toddy en route.

"I'm waiting to get a response from Toddy, before I decide when we should call on the admiral. We may have to develop some sort of mechanical problem to delay our arrival."

The Bulgarian border post was un-manned, and the barrier was raised in the open position to allow traffic to pass through. There was very little traffic on this road at this time of day, so they drove on.

"I sent Toddy a text message as we landed to say that I had an unexpected opportunity to meet him, and he said he'd be glad to meet us." Once they had signed for the vehicle, they had ensured it was fully fuelled.

Tom felt his phone ping and looked down to see a text from Toddy

COME WHEN YOU CAN FOR BREAKFAST!

"We're on!" said Tom.

18

N aomi sat in the back of the Land Rover as it headed up to White Horse Hill. She had heard about some of the bad things that had happened to Anna and Tom during the election; now she was involved in something that could turn out to be another one. Still, she thought, got to support her feisty cousin.

"If you can make a call now, you should have a good signal," said Mike. It was a short drive to Meadow Farm, so if Sonya could get away then they could pick her up by the roadside.

"Hi, Sonya its Anna, can you speak?"

"Is OK - he's watching video" came the reply. Anna wanted Sonya to sneak out of her caravan and walk towards the big hill and they would come and get her. Mike suggested that was better than blundering in.

Anna gave Mike a thumbs-up. He switched to side lights to avoid dazzling Sonya and so that their own vision would adapt to the dark. Naomi's job was to bundle Sonya into the back of the vehicle.

They edged forward along the narrow lane, the hedgerows making it seem darker. Mike reckoned it was about half a mile so he increased speed a little to close the distance between them.

They peered into the darkness for any sign of someone walking towards them.

As the lane straightened out Mike could make out the shape of the farm buildings. He indicated to Anna, who craned her neck to see a little more clearly. The side lights showed them the edge of the road and the road immediately in front of them.

They saw what looked like security lights come on illuminating the farm buildings. They also heard the sound of dogs barking.

"What's going on?" asked Naomi from behind them.

"Maybe Sonya's absence has been spotted" said Mike as he increased speed along the lane.

"There!" Anna pointed into the gloom, where she could see the outline of someone running towards them. Mike flashed the headlights of the Land Rover so that Sonya could see them.

"Better turn round" he said as he manoeuvred the vehicle to make it easier for Sonya to climb in, so they could get away quickly.

"Sonya! This way!" called Naomi as she caught sight of the running figure. As she peered into the gloom she caught sight of a shape also moving along the road.

"There's dogs chasing her!" Naomi said, incredulous. She reached out to grab Sonya and pull her into the back of the Land Rover.

As Naomi pulled her in, she heard Sonya yell. One of the dogs had caught Sonya's leg. Naomi pulled the girl in and reached down and gave the dog a punch; it gave a yelp and fell away.

"Go!" said Naomi, "she's safe inside."

Mike drove the Land Rover as quickly as the narrow lane would allow. As they drove Naomi shone her torch at Sonya.

"Leg's been bitten!" she said. "Anna's a doctor, so she can patch you up, Sonya".

They got back to Shepherds Cottage and they got Sonya inside while Anna fetched her medical bag. Naomi reassured Sonya, who was shaking, that she was safe now and that Anna would look at her leg. Sonya nodded her understanding. She looked even smaller than Anna remembered and was paler. Mike said that he would call the police and let them know what had happened.

"OK, Sonya, let's have a look at this" said Anna, as she reappeared with her medical bag.

* * *

"Nice place!" said Sid as he drove up to the front of Toddy's villa. It was still early when they arrived, but Tom had texted ahead to announce their imminent arrival. There were lights on as they parked outside. Both Tom and Sid stretched as they walked towards the house, after the long drive.

They were ushered in by one of Toddy's staff, a surly looking type. Probably not used to early starts, thought Tom as they were led into a dining room.

"Tomeee!" Toddy had lost none of his boyish enthusiasm. "All dressed up like a soldier" he added as he regarded their combat dress.

Tom introduced Sid and Toddy shook his hand like a long-lost brother. He suggested that they sit and spoke to his colleague asking for coffee and pastries to be served. The servile type withdrew, closing the door behind him.

"So!" Toddy began, "here we are! Great that you could stop by, Tom!"

Sid suppressed a smirk – if you knew the trouble we have been to so that we can just 'drop by', he thought.

Tom caught sight of an elegant carriage clock sitting on a side table. It was a useful reminder for him that they had to be heading on to Varna later in the morning, so he should get down to business as soon as breakfast was served.

"Those folks you introduced me to the last time I was here" he began. He wanted to gauge Toddy's reaction as he broached the matter of their criminality. He needed Toddy to trust him, and not to think that he was being accused, or that he had been duped. He needed a positive response, so he had to proceed gingerly.

"Great guys!" Toddy said. "They've got great plans and want me to be part of their operation."

Not the reaction I want, thought Tom, but it was in character with Toddy's boyish enthusiasm about everything. Tom recalled an episode from their time at school together.

"You remember that sports master at school?" he began. He took a bite of a pastry as he watched for Toddy's reaction. The sports master had made an advance on Toddy and had been discreetly dismissed when his proclivities were revealed.

He watched as Toddy called to mind the episode, which must have been painful.

"We all trusted him" Tom continued. "He was not who we thought he was."

This time Tom saw the dawning of a thought in Toddy's face. Sid kept perfectly still, so that his presence wouldn't be a distraction. He'd watched Tom at work like this before, when he'd been trying to turn a bad guy and bring over to the side of righteousness as Tom described it.

"You've got the land that they want to use" Tom continued. "So you've got something they want, and you can choose who you do business with" he added. "Have you signed anything?"

"Nothing in writing..." Toddy began.

"If they've misrepresented themselves, it's fraudulent" said Tom, "The Brits are wanted men in the UK. If you go in with them, you'll be arrested the next time you come over to see your family anywhere in the UK."

"I'm bound by honour -" Toddy began. Tom cut him off with the sort of gesture a parent gives to a slightly naughty child.

"They are dishonouring you" said Tom gently but insistently. "They do not deserve your respect or your trust."

He didn't want Toddy to feel like he had been made a fool of, but rather that he had been misled by a bunch of schemers.

"Nobody will blame you if you back away from this deal, before it's too late" he added.

"You came a long way to tell me this" said Toddy, Tom could see that he was still processing the implications of what he had been told. He needed to nudge him further into acceptance.

"If you want to stand for public office, you can do so as someone who stands up to organized crime and all of the bad things that can happen when good people do nothing."

This was the point where Tom had to back off. It was up to Toddy to understand that there was a way out of his predicament. The only sound in the room was the ticking of the clock.

"You will help me do this, Tom?"

19

Naomi was astonished at the sight before her. They were back in Shepherds Cottage and Mike was dispensing brandy for all, as an antidote to shock, on Anna's orders. After her encounter with the dog, Naomi knocked her brandy back and held out her glass for a refill. Mike gave her a wink as he did the honours.

Anna had attended to Sonya's leg, which was now stretched out on a chair. The dog bite needed cleaning and stitching, which Anna did without fuss, as Sonya had looked on impassively. The effect of the shock was beginning to wear off and Sonya began to grimace as the pain from her leg asserted itself.

"No time to waste, Sonya, I needed to clean you up right smartly" said Anna as she reached into her medicine bag and found a packet of tablets and shook some into her hand. "Take those with your brandy" she said. "Make you sleep well!" she added, only half joking.

"Wow, Anna!" said Naomi, "That was epic!"

Naomi had heard stories from Anna's time working at A & E in Glasgow and knew she could be feisty in a tight spot. She had heard about her narrow escape when someone threw acid at her in the election campaign; but they'd just rescued someone from a very bad place.

"Thanks to you and Mike we managed to pull it off" said Anna with a smile, as she was putting her medical implements away. "You gave that dog a right good *doin'* and Mike's a *canny driver right enough!*"

Naomi blinked in disbelief at her wee cousin who was on the short side, and pregnant too. As a fitness instructor she had learnt about self-defence to keep herself fit, so punching the dog was an instinctive thing to do.

"Glad to help!" she said, as she felt the benefit of the brandy.

They heard the sound of a car pulling into the drive. Mike got up to check that it wasn't one of the bad guys who might have followed them.

"Police" he announced. He'd met Detective Inspector Izzy Bannister before, so he went to the door to let her in. Naomi, who thought of herself as a free spirit was ready to spring to the defence of her doctor cousin who had just performed an amazing act, and the flatfoots were probably going to tell her off for doing their job.

"Evening all" said Izzy, walking into the kitchen. "Nice to be back! Where's the patient?"

Close behind Izzy came another plain-clothes policeman who introduced himself as Detective Sergeant John Moran.

Naomi took in the slight figure of Izzy Bannister who gave her a smile. Those bright brown eyes probably don't miss much, she thought. DS John Moran on the other hand had ice-blue eyes that seemed to look straight through her. Interesting, she thought.

Izzy was all business. After she introduced herself to Sonya she said that she would like 'a little chat' about what had just happened, and how it was that Sonya found herself in this situation.

"We know these folks quite well but they've always been too clever to get caught" said DS Moran. "With your help, Sonya, we can put them away for a long time." Sonya's gaze was fixed on his face as he spoke. I saw him first, thought Naomi as she watched them both.

"You might need a witness statement, if you want to take down my particulars" Naomi said feeling the benefit of the brandy. DS Moran gave her a nod and a smile. Perfect, she thought.

Meanwhile Izzy had been chatting to Sonya, and they agreed that she should stay put until some sort of accommodation could be arranged, but she would have to go to the police station and give a statement about her experience.

"Looks like you're thriving, Anna," said Izzy. "How's Tom getting on? I saw there was some more nonsense recently." She was referring to the Oxford Info affair.

"Tom is away just now" Anna replied, "as he's been asked to help in a certain matter...." Izzy nodded her understanding. Need to know.

"Your friend has been causing trouble, Don" Darren's voice the phone was cold. Don was sitting in his favourite beach tavern in Kyrenia. The warm breeze and the glint of the sun on the water were at odds with the chill he felt from the voice on the phone.

"Which friend would that be?" he asked guilelessly. He had been warned by text that Tom had recently met Toddy, thanks to the good offices of one of Toddy's retainers who he had paid well for information.

"Scobie" came the reply, "paid a visit to Toddy the other day and I'm sure he was up to no good."

"Do you know what they discussed?" Johnson was trying to

work out what Darren's angle was going to be. He hoped to avoid any delay to the plans he was formulating with his new Bulgarian friends.

"My sources were unable to discover what they spoke about, but there were two of them. I didn't discover who the other one was."

"They were at the same school, so it could be a friendly visit?" Don suggested.

"An MP doesn't get away from Parliament while it's in session, so there's something going on, Don. I suggest that you make it your business to find out what."

Don was momentarily stunned - he was being *warned*. Well, he could easily contrive a reason to pay a return visit to Varna, but he needed to keep an eye on the costs of travel.

"Leave him to me, Darren, I'll get to the bottom of this" Don said. He hoped that he sounded convincing.

"Just remember, Don....." Darren's voice was metallic on the phone. "My friends have a lot riding on this development. Anything or anyone that gets in the way...."

"Understood" said Don. He wanted to get Darren off the phone on good terms, but Darren had other ideas.

"Watch your step, Don, these people don't like the idea that they've been made fools of."

After the end of the call, Don put the phone back into his pocket and picked up his glass and took a long swig. He had never got on with Tom Scobie while he was his constituency agent. Their paths crossed when Tom won the nomination as the candidate, but Don's loyalty was to Charles Markham who had rescued him from possible ruin. So he understood loyalty.

"Meester Don?" Don was shaken out of his thoughts by the unlikely sight of an orthodox priest, complete with a sort of black head cover.

"May I join you?" the stranger said, as he sat down opposite.

Don pulled himself into a more upright posture, partly out of respect for the reverend gentlemen, and partly in case he had to leave in a hurry.

"Good afternoon, sir, to what do I owe the pleasure?" Don thought it was always good to play up the formal Englishman act when in doubt.

"My name is Father Peter," said the stranger. "You have some friends who are worried about you."

Everybody wants to be my friend, thought Don, this could be interesting. Father Peter's smile seemed genuine. Not a killer, thought Don.

"I am happy to find you and I am able to give you a message" he continued.

Don sat a little more upright. Who wanted to send him a message and how had he been so easy to find? He needed to understand a bit more about Father Peter before he took matters much further.

"I'm forgetting my manners" Don's tone became more emollient. "Can I offer you something?" Father Peter was happy to have a cup of coffee, which Don ordered.

"I am not the police" continued Father Peter, as he waited for his coffee to arrive.

"Glad to hear it!" Don laughed despite the unsettling turn the conversation was taking. Why was every conversation so difficult?

"You are troubled?" It was as if Father Peter could read his thoughts. He should keep his guard up.

"I'm a businessman, and there is much on my mind." He hoped that was a plausible response. He was gratified to see Father Peter nod in acknowledgement.

"Much trouble in the world" said Father Peter, as his coffee arrived.

"Er, which of my friends has sent you?" asked Don, seeking

to get to the heart of the matter. He wanted to make sure this chap was not some holy Joe who thought he was a soft touch for a donation to the local monastery.

"Mr Scobie sends you his best wishes." Don was sipping his wine and managed not to choke as he heard the words. "He is happy to meet you and see if there is something you both can do, that will help you both" continued Father Peter.

Intriguing, thought Don.

20

"Let's see how he reacts to the offer," said Tom.

They were back in the kitchen at Shepherds Cottage after Tom and Sid had slipped over to Bulgaria under the guise of being part of a NATO exercise. He had contacted his cousin Matt to see if he could use his back-channel network of clergy to send a message to Don.

"Always leave people with a way out" replied Matt down a fuzzy phone line. He had been travelling in the same region as Tom and had made the suggestion when they had managed to speak on the phone. Tom had been in the middle of a high-level briefing with the US admiral in charge of the exercise when he saw that Matt was calling, so had to contrive a reason to escape and call back.

"I've sent the same message to Toddy," said Tom. "Help us nail the bad guys and I can help you with your political ambitions."

"A bit different with Don" said Matt. "Help us and we'll try to keep you out of jail if your Russian friends don't kill you first!"

"Don was courtesy itself to my orthodox colleague" said Matt. "Father Peter saw the fear in his eyes. He'd just been on the phone to someone and it didn't seem like a friendly chat with a mate."

Matt had explained to Tom that Father Peter had done some useful work in Lebanon talking to warring militias and also in Cyprus on cross-border talks between communities on either side of the dividing line.

"More joy in heaven over the sinner that repenteth..." said Matt.

"I just hope that I can do a good job persuading the Serious Fraud Office that Toddy will be of greater value out of jail than inside" said Tom. "They seemed a little too keen to grab him from what my friend Adam told me."

He had watched Toddy's reaction as he traced the possible connections between his business acquaintances and the Markham network that Don now controlled. He needed to be sure that Toddy hadn't gone over to the dark side in pursuit of his own self-aggrandisement. He also needed to preserve Toddy's own sense of his own importance.

"If *we* can do this together, Toddy, you will be a real hero, and people will respect you for the right reasons" Tom had said.

Toddy's expression had been neutral, but Tom could see in his eyes that he didn't like to be made a fool of. Almost imperceptibly he had nodded his head, as if making his mind up. Tom saw his countenance change as he gave him a conspiratorial smile.

"I just need to get you and Don Johnson in the same locality," said Matt.

* * *

"You are not like police back home, all bad and hit you always," said Sonya.

She was sitting in the interview suite in the police station where people were interviewed who had been victims of abuse or worse. Izzy and DS Moran were sitting across a low table with coffee and biscuits for them all.

"Well, Sonya, we want to make sure that the people who brought you here cannot do the same to other girls like you." Izzy's smile was genuine. She had come to admire Sonya's pluck in calling Anna and sneaking out while her minder was watching a video.

"Men are bad but women are worse" Sonya said, looking small as she sat wrapped in an oversized down jacket. "Trick me to sign papers and take my passport."

Izzy made a note, she would need to speak to the immigration authorities about getting Sonya some identification papers.

"Promise me paradise and good job in fashion house….." As Sonya continued, she began to sob. "All lies and no future for me now!"

She explained that she had been recruited by a lady looking for ambitious girls who wanted to work in the fashion world as models. They would be going to London or Paris, so Sonya had jumped at the chance. Then she was told that her family would have to pay for her ticket, which she could pay back from her wages. At every stage Izzy asked for names and dates if Sonya could remember.

"We'll go to the farm where you were kept and talk to the people there and most likely arrest them" said Izzy. She saw Sonya smile at this news. "Is good!" she said, brightening up.

"I tell my family what happen and they will not be happy with me" she said, as her face fell at the thought. "I got no job."

Shattered dreams thought Izzy; well, maybe some good can come out of this. DS Moran picked up the plate of biscuits and offered it to Sonya who took one and started munching as Izzy was writing in her notebook. Izzy waved away the biscuits so DS Moran took one as well and gave Sonya a conspiratorial smile.

"Did we interview the Pascoes about the incident with Tom Scobie and his brother being run off the road during the election?" she asked.

"I'll need to look, but that matter was dealt with by other officers" he replied. There had been several officers removed from investigating Markham, so it didn't surprise Izzy that the matter hadn't been followed up.

"Perhaps we should pay them a call," said Izzy. "We've got statements from Tom and his brother, or we should have" she said.

"What happen to me now?" asked Sonya.

* * *

"Oi! Charlie boy, you got a visitor" Markham hated being called Charlie, but he smiled at the prison warder. It was Stevie, one of his new mates, who he had been able to cultivate. After his conviction, Markham had seen to it that he could reach out to his network beyond the prison walls. He needed to access his emergency fund and use it to bribe people and open doors.

"That journalist again" said Stevie as they walked across the open courtyard to the visitors' block near the gate. Markham nodded his understanding; Scobie had a journalist on his team, and Markham had got several on his.

"You're looking well!" said Gordon. "The new regime agrees with you" he added with a smirk.

"Not getting enough exercise" replied Markham grumpily. "I think I need one of those exercise bikes."

Markham didn't think that their conversation was being bugged, but he didn't want to take the chance. Gordon was one of his channels to the outside world, which he wanted to keep open. Speaking in oblique terms was something they'd quickly worked out.

"Your friend has been very busy, but he might be getting a little careless," said Gordon. Markham knew he was referring to Don. "He's beginning to attract attention and Scobie was able to meet a mutual acquaintance of his in Bulgaria" he added.

Markham tried to recall the acquaintance referred to. He had lived all his life on his wits by paying attention to details. "Ah yes!" he said, "the old school chum." He was gratified to see a nod in response.

"The first thing to do is to discredit Scobie," said Markham.

"The real danger is that the school chum and your friend come to the attention of the authorities in Bulgaria" replied Gordon. He didn't think there was any point in pursuing a vendetta against Tom Scobie, as there was only so much he could do now that he was an MP. He was a public figure now, so he'd have to watch his step.

"Just indulge me on this" continued Markham. "A bit of trouble with the constituency association, and some rumours inside the Party, that sort of thing."

"I'll see what I can do about pulling a few strings" came the reply.

Markham had built up his network based on patronage. The beneficiaries needed to be reminded that although he was temporarily indisposed he could still use their support, or he would send them a reminder.

21

"What a lovely house!" said Don. His reaction to Toddy's villa was genuine. "I didn't get a look around when we were last here" he added.

Darren's smile was a little more synthetic, as he listened to Toddy explaining how his family had been thrown out of the house when the communists took over. He had got used to Toddy's gushing style of dealing with people, which he found endearing and annoying at the same time.

Toddy had readily agreed to Don's suggestion that they meet to consider their future plans. He was aware of Tom's warning about being involved with these folks, but he wanted to make his own mind up. There was a lot of money at stake for them all.

"Let's go and sit down" Toddy said finally after they had walked around the house. Don thought that Toddy would make a good estate agent by the way he showed off the property. He led them into a comfortable looking room with sofas and side tables.

"Drinks?" suggested Toddy. They both accepted whiskies and sat down with him around a coffee table covered with glossy magazines.

They heard footsteps coming down the stairs and in walked a glamorous blonde dressed in a tight dress. Don's eyes were drawn to her figure which Darren noticed. Easily led, he thought. She gave them all a friendly wave and told Toddy that she was going into town. He blew her a kiss and turned back to the others.

"Charming" said Don. Toddy smiled at the compliment, and Darren kept his fixed smile and said nothing. He decided to get things started.

"Toddy, we're very excited at the project that we're going to work on together" he said. He was watching Toddy's face to measure his reaction. He was pleased to see the favourable response. "We're all going to be very rich thanks to the land you own, Toddy, and the beachfront that we can turn into a classy resort." He was laying on the upside of their working together, as his Russian backers wanted access to the real estate.

"But let me ask you something, Toddy" said Darren with a detectable edge to his voice. Don noticed that Toddy's expression seemed to freeze, as if he was expecting to hear something unpleasant. "My friends are a little bit concerned about some of your friends, except of course Don here." Darren turned towards Don, who managed to smile and nod sagely as if accepting the compliment.

Toddy managed to maintain a poker-faced expression, meaning that Darren would have to elaborate. Don thought this was a smart move. Someone less sure of himself would have started blurting out something about not wanting to spoil the deal and disowning whoever it was that was the problem.

"You and Don both have Tom Scobie in common, and he is a troublemaker" Darren continued. Toddy took a sip of his whisky and made a dismissive gesture.

"I can't see how one person can put the whole project at risk" he said. Darren was going to have to spell out the problem and the solution.

"Don can tell you just how much mischief Scobie can cause" Darren said, giving Don a meaningful look. It was Don's turn to take a swig of his whisky while he thought of the best way to tell his story. Toddy decided that he didn't like the way the conversation was going and while Don was involved with his drink he jumped in first.

"OK, Don and Darren...." As he began to speak he sat forward in his chair. "This is *my* country, I know *my* people. Russians, Turks and others, they come and go. Brits – I'm half British, don't forget, we do commerce where we can with who we can."

Don noted that Darren was tapping his finger against his glass, waiting to hear what Toddy had to say.

"You think I don't know what Tom's game is? He was here a couple of weeks ago sitting where you are." He was looking squarely at Darren, and glancing at Don. Obviously he thinks Darren is the big fish here, thought Don, wondering how he could get a word in.

"I think I can trust my own judgement, chaps" Toddy continued. "That includes what I say to Tom Scobie and also who I choose to do business with." Don noticed that Darren's expression had hardened, he was not used to being spoken down to.

"Let's be clear" continued Toddy, "this is strictly business, not personal. If you don't want to do business with me, then others will."

"I think that is a reasonable position, Toddy." Don had finally caught up with the sense of the conversation. "So long as we all know where we stand." He caught a glimpse of Darren's disapproving expression from the corner of his eye. He was going to have to remind Darren that Toddy was sitting on prime real estate and they needed him for this project to work.

* * *

"Well, that was interesting!" said Don as their car drove them away from Toddy's villa. "All friends now!" he added, sensing Darren's displeasure at having had the wind knocked out of his sails by Toddy.

"We'll see" Darren said sourly. "We're going to have to convince our Russki friends that Toddy is reliable."

"We can manage Toddy, as long as he can see the money at the end of the tunnel" said Don, not quite comfortable with the metaphor. "We just have to rattle the can so he can hear the coins tinkling. Leave Scobie to me." He gave Darren a sideways glance: "My old boss has got him covered."

"Your old boss is in jail and Scobie helped to put him there" Darren sneered. Don had to acknowledge this.

"We've learnt how Scobie operates and the one chink in his armour is his reputation" he said. "I think that we can separate Toddy from Scobie once he realizes that his old school chum is no use to him, because he's damaged goods."

"OK, let's see how that goes" said Darren as they drove along the coast road back into Varna.

Don allowed the thought to stay unanswered. He needed to get hold of Markham and see where this particular campaign had got to. He knew that Markham had a muckraking journalist on the payroll – if he was getting paid these days.

"Thing is, Don" said Darren in a matter-of-fact voice "the Russkis can deal with Toddy, 'cos he's Bulgarian and they know how to deal with them. They want what he's got - which is the real estate" he added. Don felt a 'but' coming along, one he wouldn't like.

"You want to buy into this deal, or your boss does" added Darren. "You've got a small pot of cash you want to invest, but it is small beer alongside what the Russkis are going to put in."

Don tried to keep his expression neutral but he knew the truth of what Darren had just said. He needed to put Markham's cash somewhere and this looked like a surefire bet. But he would be the junior partner. He also knew that Markham would be keeping score of his investments against the day he managed to get out of jail, by hook or by crook.

"So to summarize, Don" added Darren "*we* don't need *you* or *him*."

Don gave Darren what he thought was a knowing smile, as if to say: I'll show you, matey. In his mind he recalled that Father Peter had given him a card as he left their meeting. He thought about what was written; *This day I call the heavens and the earth as witnesses against you that I have set before you life and death, blessings and curses. Now choose life, so that you and your children may live.*

22

A nother day at the office, thought Tom as he walked across Westminster Bridge towards Portcullis House. The autumn sun cast a warm glow over the Palace of Westminster even if the wind was cold. He had been signing papers in the offices of the law firm that represented Oxford Info, of which he was still a director. The recent episode with the company required some adjustments to shareholdings that needed his signature.

He had sent a message to the committee chairman and the clerk explaining that he would be late for the session that morning, but in the event the paperwork had been quite quickly taken care of. He slid into his seat in the committee room with a nod to the chairman, having collected his papers from the office.

In an idle moment Tom flicked through his diary thinking about the dates of the next recess. He was also wondering when mini-Scobie would put in an appearance. As he flicked the pages he saw a note for this coming Friday. It was the date of their wedding anniversary.

He let out an involuntary groan which attracted the attention of his colleagues. He felt himself flush with embarrassment as he made a gesture to signify that all was well. As the session went on he realised that the recent share transactions involving Oxford Info resulted in him having some extra funds available. There was time for him to get Anna something sparkly for their anniversary.

"Are you OK?" It was Kat who caught him on the way out of the meeting as it adjourned.

"Fancy a shopping trip? I've got to get something, and a woman's perspective would be welcome." He looked at her archly.

"Not the sort of proposition that a woman expects to get, but why not?" she replied. "Our whip doesn't begin until mid-afternoon" she added, explaining that MPs were required to be available to vote from the time stated on their daily note from the whips' office.

"Meet you in New Palace Yard in ten minutes?" he said as they went off to their respective offices. He was glad that he had remembered; and the windfall was a bonus.

They decided to go out through the gates of New Palace Yard, rather than wait for a taxi to come in. As they walked up the footpath Tom glanced around him. He could think of worse places to work.

"We'll get a passing cab on the street" he said. He waved at several passing black cabs but they were all taken. Eventually Kat spotted a cab with its 'for hire' light on.

Putting her fingers into her mouth she let out a piercing whistle that would have woken the dead in Westminster Abbey.

"My brother taught me that trick" she said as they piled into the cab.

Kat suggested Bond Street, to which Tom agreed, seeing the price of his little gift going up.

"Like school kids playing truant!" said Kat, enjoying their temporary freedom. They got out of the cab and walked along the street looking at the passers-by with their bags displaying the name of famous and expensive brands.

"I hope you're not leading me astray, Ms Quinlan" he said, as much to himself as to Kat.

She pointed at a shop with glistening things in the window and pressed the buzzer to enable them to go inside. The sales assistant was appropriately helpful, as she knew this would be a sale. Tom suggested a bracelet would be appropriate, hoping to keep the price at a manageable level.

"Look at this one" said Kat, holding up a rather gaudy creation.

"It's what all the oligarchs' mistresses are wearing!" said Tom. Kat laughed.

He spotted something that he thought would go with Anna's eyes, so he asked to see it and asked for the price quickly, before Kat could suggest that he buy it. In the event it was within his comfort level. While they were examining it, the sales assistant let someone else in, as she saw that this sale was about to complete.

Kat held up the bracelet to admire it and made some ooh-ing noises.

As she did so a camera flash went off. The other person turned out to be an enterprising photographer who had managed to grab a snap of them both in a jewellery store, with Kat in rapture at the sight of the bracelet.

"Push off!" she yelled at him. He beat a hasty retreat.

"So sorry! I thought he was a customer," said the sales assistant.

"That's going to be trouble," said Tom.

* * *

Tom was looking forward to another meeting with Adam from the security services. They had agreed to meet off the parliamentary estate, as there were too many eyes and ears that might not be friendly. Adam was happier with meetings held over a lunch nearby. He had put yesterday's incident with the photographer out of his mind. He wanted to concentrate on this meeting.

Tom had made his mind up that the effort should be put into bringing Toddy over to the side of righteousness instead of trying to gather evidence for a prosecution. The bigger fish was Don, who was a British national and directly involved in wrongdoing. Somehow Toddy might be persuaded to bring Don to a place where he could be arrested. He now needed to persuade Adam and his colleagues to agree to this course of action.

As usual Adam was waiting for him in a corner seat at the back of the restaurant where he could see who came and went. He waved Tom to an adjacent seat so that they sat at right angles to each other so they were both able to look around the room. A bottle of red wine was on the table.

As they ordered, Tom brought Adam up to date on how he had visited Toddy whilst on a NATO exercise, and also managed to get a message to Don via the good offices of his cousin Matt and his network of clergy who were in the reconciliation business.

Adam was impressed - or he appeared to be. Tom wanted him to know that he had his own way of reaching people.

"Surely the aim of this exercise is to bag the big fish. Neither Toddy nor Don are big fish, they are the sprats we need to catch the mackerel" said Tom as they drank a glass of wine together.

"To get to the real bad guys is going to require some international liaison with foreign services and law and order agencies" Adam replied. "More people in the know."

"It's a bigger prize, to unravel a whole network and grab the proceeds of crime" continued Tom, warming to his theme.

"I'll need to speak to my superiors about this, as it will involve several agencies; but I can see the attraction," said Adam.

"We can start with Toddy" continued Tom. "I can see that he is attracted to the idea that money can buy him what he wants, and he really wants a sense of restitution, for the sake of his family honour. This is a big part of his life that he heard about from his uncles and aunts, as well as his parents. He will be the one to restore the family estates."

"Reparation" he added, as an afterthought.

"Even if they are mortgaged to a bunch of dodgy villains?" asked Adam.

Tom made a face. He recognised the challenge of bring Toddy over. He was not entirely sure that he had managed to convince him during their last meeting.

"I've got my investigative journalist contact on the trail of Don's money" said Tom, hoping to inject a positive note into the conversation. "If we can persuade him that his pot of money is unsafe, we might be able to draw him to a place where we can arrest him. But we'll need local police assistance."

"Your investigative journalist?" asked Adam. "Is she any good?" Tom nodded "She's very resourceful" he said. "Helped to put Markham behind bars".

"We're all in favour of any legitimate means of serving justice, Tom" Adam said trying to regain control of the conversation. "We've got to be able to present evidence to a jury, remember."

"Ideally, we can enable Toddy to serve his community as an MP with clean hands and allow him the satisfaction of redeeming his family's reputation."

"And Don?" asked Adam.

Tom took a sip of his wine. He wanted to be able to put an

end to the nagging feeling that his whole life was haunted by Markham and his cronies. If he could get Don behind bars it would send a message to those holdouts who were still in the thrall of Markham. Better still if he could remove the funds which kept Markham operating even though he was behind bars himself.

"Don is in a difficult position" said Tom as their lunch arrived. "The people he is trying to get into business with won't hesitate to remove him if they think he's a threat to their operation."

Adam nodded his understanding.

"He's managed to involve himself in a deal that would see a development on the land owned by Toddy and his family, with Don and his partners taking a good share of the revenues from the project. So he's basically a broker, a middle man who could be got rid of."

"And Toddy?"

"He's getting mixed up in something he doesn't fully understand" said Tom, tucking into his food. "He hasn't really got any legal advice, he's flying by the seat of his pants."

"Dangerous?"

"Deadly dangerous"

23

Why Did You Let My Daughter Die?

The headline on the front of the tabloid paper was below a photo of Tom and Kat in the jeweller's shop. The caption suggested that 'Blond cutie Kat shopping with her new best friend Tom Scobie' were enjoying the high life in Westminster. Alongside it was a grainy picture of Ivana who had been Tom's interpreter in the Balkans. The story related to the death of Tom's interpreter after he had left the Balkans. She was stalked and killed as an act of revenge by some of the people Tom had been trying to bring to justice.

"Wow!" said Amy as they stood in Tom's Westminster office. He had been called in the small hours by the Party press office when the story broke, and shortly afterwards by Mu from the constituency after the local press had called her for comment. He had called Anna to warn her; she had suggested that the 'numpty' who wrote the story had better not come near her.

Tom knew that something was coming after the photographer had caught him and Kat in the jewellery shop but he hadn't expected this angle on the story. He had not been approached before the story was printed. Normally the paper would call for a comment even though they were going to run the story. Tom smelt a very big rat and could guess who was behind this.

"Did you ever meet Ivana's family?" asked Amy. The story was a complaint by someone purporting to be Ivana's father. He blamed Tom for the death of his daughter.

"No, we never spoke about things outside of the job" he said, although he recalled her musing about what life could be like when there was peace in that land.

"I liked her of course, she had a wicked sense of humour and took the mickey out of what she called the big boys".

"Shame" said Amy.

"Welcome to the world of politics," said Tom. "Churchill said that politics was more dangerous than war, because in war you can only be killed once, but in politics many times." He watched as Amy processed the idea and saw her nod her understanding.

"Sad" she said.

He would have to produce a statement relating to the sad events surrounding Ivana's death and explain that he had been shopping for an anniversary present and wanted a woman's opinion about his choice. That should shut down any rumour that the two of them were having an affair.

His phone rang; he saw it was Kat. "What a rotten thing to do!" she said as soon as he answered. "It's that vile cretin who was giving you the evils in the chamber the other day" she added. "I'm going to complain to the Speaker, Tom; shall we make a joint approach?" She sounded like she was walking along a street somewhere.

"Yes, let's ask for an appointment" he said.

"Better still, are you in for PMQs today?" she asked. "I'll raise a point of order, 'cos he'll be in the gallery. I can use parliamentary privilege to name him."

"Good idea" said Tom. "I'll be there!"

Another call, it was Mu. "How do, Mu?" Tom tried to sound jovial. He wasn't surprised to hear her tell him that one of the old Markham gang of supporters had called asking if there could be an EGM at the weekend to consider the conduct of the MP.

"Here we go again" he said. "Usual suspects?" Mu agreed. It would hopefully be a question of facing down the malcontents - something he could do without.

"Let's bounce them" he said. "I can get away tonight and we can convene tomorrow evening".

Mu agreed that this was a good idea and she would ring around some of Tom's supporters and warn them to be ready to see off any votes of no confidence.

They ended the call and Tom plonked himself down in his chair. Amy saw his drained expression "Coffee?" she suggested, as that was Tom's usual pick-me-up. He nodded wearily "Have we got any brandy?"

"A bit early, Mr Scobie!" she replied with mock ferocity. She was glad to see him smile at the reproach. "Besides, you don't want to go into the chamber smelling of bevvy!"

In the event, Mr Speaker acknowledged the point raised by Kat and motioned to the press gallery and suggested that the gentleman concerned should sit down and have a nice cup of tea with the honourable lady and resolve any misunderstandings.

"He won't misunderstand me when I get hold of him!" said Kat as they left the chamber.

* * *

"The pot of gold at the end of the rainbow? We're all looking for that, Tom!"

Georgina took a sip of her coffee as she and Tom were

looking at a diagram of Markham's financial dealings. It was originally drawn up by her colleague Jack, who had been on the trail of Markham and who had been killed by one of his henchmen in a hit-and-run late one evening.

Tom had called Georgina to let her know that he would be available on Thursday morning as he had other matters to attend to that day. She had agreed to meet and to provide the coffee and croissants. She had discovered that Tom was partial to the occasional pastry.

"I don't think that Don would be able to re-arrange everything in a hurry, especially after Markham's assets were seized, but there must be enough to keep financing the operation" she added.

Tom tapped the paper with a pencil. "There must be a way into this. Don needs something he can use to brag his way into a big deal in the Black Sea resort business."

"We need to show him that we know where the money is. If he thinks that his own little nest egg is not safe, maybe he'll be more co-operative", Georgie nodded her understanding. "Has the girl been able to shed any light on things?" she asked.

"Sonya? I need to ask Izzy if she's got anything useful that she can share with us. This is a police investigation so she'll have to be careful" he said.

Tom looked around to see if anybody could overhear them. They were in the anonymous office on a trading estate outside Didcot, where the investigative agency Georgina ran was based, at arm's length from her publisher.

Georgina followed his gaze. "We're all sworn to secrecy here, Tom" she said. "But I think there's someone who might be able to help" she said as she got up and walked over to a desk.

Tom followed her as she tapped a colleague on the shoulder. "This is Gloria. If anyone can find a needle in a haystack, she can. Also, she's been working on the Sonya case, so until we get anything from the police she can help us on this particular matter."

"Well, Gloria" Tom began. "Once upon a time....."

* * *

For the EGM, later that evening, Mu had booked a room upstairs at the Rifleman, a pub they all used for official and unofficial meetings. When Tom arrived, he wasn't surprised to see a group of sour-faced folks sitting together nursing their glasses of wine or beer.

"We have the right number of people to be quorate" said Mu conspiratorially, meaning that the meeting could proceed according to the rules. Tom nodded and glanced around the room, smiling at the sour-faced group which had sat at the back of the room, putting chairs between them and the table that Mu had commandeered for the meeting.

Tom knew that this bunch were the irreconcilables, he would never win them over. They were small in number, but well organised. No doubt Markham had been in touch with them. He needed to identify the go-between who passed messages, but that was for another day.

"Can we begin, madam chairman?" asked one of the group, a pasty-faced man with a dodgy comb-over, "I believe that we have enough people here to open the meeting."

"Let me just check the time" replied Mu. "The meeting was called for 6:30 and it's just 6:25 pm" she said in a tone that managed to be both patronising and sarcastic at the same time. For the benefit of those who doubted her word she indicated the clock on the wall.

The sour expressions on the faces of the group began to show alarm as they heard the sound of footsteps coming along the corridor. A merry bunch came into the room equipped with glasses and bags of crisps. They settled themselves in the front row, left vacant by the others, with much clinking of glasses and rustling of crisp wrappers.

"Are you sitting comfortably?" asked Mu.

24

"Digitisation!" said Gloria. Her smile lit up the dull office they were sitting in. Georgina had called Tom, encouraging him to come over as soon as he could. He managed to escape the House of Commons and drove down to Didcot one wet evening.

"Gloria has found a needle!" Georgina began. "Not sure that it's the right needle but let's see" she said as they walked down a corridor. They found Gloria at her cubicle working away at her computer.

She quickly explained to them that she had gone back through the material that had originally been unearthed by Jack. A lot of it was in accounts that were in the process of being transferred from old- fashioned filing cabinets to more modern digital versions.

"I got lucky and tried a few possible password combinations" she explained, giving Georgina a sideways look, as if she was seeking approval to reveal some of the magic.

"We have a programme that can crack passwords" explained Georgina. "But we don't advertise that" she said, giving Tom a stare that was intended to swear him to silence. He made a zipping gesture across his lips.

"Donald took over Markham's offshore account as he was a proxy for him" Gloria continued. "We can get so far, but not all the way into it because there is another level of protection which Donald has probably altered when he took over".

"So we know the account number and we know its code name" Georgina continued. "We don't know how much is in it but we can track the payments out and in".

"Payments in?" said Tom. "Who is paying into the account?"

"There are interest payments from other investments" Gloria continued "and I imagine there are still some people who pay protection money."

"So he is still getting money?" said Tom.

"I'm still working up a list of the people paying, so we can go and see them" Gloria said with a slight smile. "What is it that got them trapped by his web, I wonder?"

"Penny for them, Tom," said Georgina. She could see that his thoughts had wandered away from their discussion.

"I'm just wondering what would happen if we told Don that we knew where his pot of gold was, and how he might react" he said almost to himself.

"He's the custodian" said Georgina, following his line of thought. "His job is to safeguard Markham's millions. If that was threatened, he'd have to move it somewhere else."

"Let me speak to some of my banking friends" Georgina said. "I have someone in mind, who has dabbled in the dark side, but has since come over to the side of righteousness"

Tom looked surprised. "Lunch in the City?"

"No, he's in an open prison but it's full of white-collar criminals so it's quite cushy!" she said with a smile. "You might enjoy a visit with me."

* * *

"How are you feeling?" asked Naomi. She had just finished working through a yoga session with Anna.

It was great having Tom back early in the week; he and Mike had gone off to the constituency office.

"Fine, I think" came the reply. "It was better last time, I'm a bit more tired now". They both knew the importance of taking time to understand how Anna was really feeling rather than shrugging off aches and pains.

They were on the floor of the small sitting room in Shepherds Cottage, which entailed shifting some furniture to make space for the exercises they did together. Naomi helped Anna up off the floor and waved her towards the kitchen.

Anna sat down in her favourite chair that enabled her to look at the garden, which was looking very autumnal. She closed her eyes and listened to the sounds as Naomi replaced the furniture. Her sharp hearing heard the sound of tyres on the gravel driveway outside.

"I'll go!" she heard Naomi call as she walked down the hall. "Well! Look who's here!" she said as she led DS Moran into the kitchen. Anna couldn't help noticing Naomi's beaming smile.

"Come to protect the damsels in distress?" Naomi smiled, as she pulled out a chair for him.

"Good morning, ladies" he said, trying not to smile. "This is just a follow-up visit, so no need to panic" he added.

"Nice to see you again," said Anna. Naomi noticed that her smile was a little forced. "Can we offer you something?"

He accepted a coffee and Naomi set to work. The girls each had a herbal tea, something Anna had got used to despite sharing Tom's addiction to coffee. She knew she should moderate her intake of caffeine.

"Just thought you might like an update on how Sonya is

getting on" he began. "She's been very helpful with our inquiries" he continued.

"What's going to happen to her?" asked Anna.

"It's up to the immigration folks, but we're going to recommend she gets leave to remain, so she can help us unpick the network that brought her here."

"Sounds encouraging," said Anna. "How is she?" She had suggested that Sonya get a thorough medical examination, having initially seen how pale she was when she saw her in the pub.

"You were right on that one, doctor" he said. "She is anaemic, but now she's on a regime to build her strength up."

"She's been through a lot" Anna said. He nodded his agreement and outlined how Sonya had come to be up on the Downs in a caravan.

"She's from Albania" he began. "Was trafficked to Greece via Corfu and then over land to the UK in the back of several trucks."

"Grim!" said Naomi, as she sat down and pushed a tray across the table towards him.

"Her passport and phone were taken off her, but she was able to get her phone back" he continued. "She said that she would be expected to let her family know how she was getting on. She won the trust of the people who were moving her, and eventually the next lot didn't even know she had a phone."

"Smart kid!" said Naomi. "That's what I call presence of mind".

"So she was able to call you when she saw the opportunity" he added. "We've been up to see the Pascoe brothers with a search warrant. We found a whole bunch of passports and other ID cards, so they've been charged with the possession of false documents."

"But they're not false" said Anna, "just stolen from the people they belong to."

"Correct" he nodded. "But for now this is a holding charge. They are on bail. If we can reunite the papers with the people they belong to, we can charge them with trafficking. They'll go down for a long stretch for that!" he said, reaching for a cookie on a plate.

"Do I need to give evidence?" asked Naomi with a wide smile. DS Moran was midway through chewing his cookie and he looked directly at her as he wiped his lips.

"There's a very strong possibility" he said, trying to keep a straight face.

* * *

"Always better after a cup of your coffee, Mu!" said Tom. They were sitting in the small garret room at the top of the constituency office in Wandage.

Muriel Makepeace was Tom's constituency agent and had been instrumental in helping him to secure the candidacy in the general election. She now presided over the office and helped to keep Tom on top of matters locally.

"I'm glad you were able to get away, Tom" she smiled as she poured another cup for Mike, who acted as Tom's driver when he was around the constituency.

"So am I!" said Mike as he helped himself to a shortbread finger on the plate Muriel had put out for them.

"I think things have settled down after the recent episode" she said, referring to the EGM. "A couple of the Bandits have come into apologise" she added with a smile. "Looks like we're beginning to win them over".

"Maybe now is the time for a charm offensive," said Tom. "We've still got Henry's list of Bandits, so maybe we can peel them off one by one." This was a technique that he had used in the Balkans to bring over some of the small fry in the criminal gangs he and his team were pursuing.

"Christmas is coming" said Mike as he reached for another piece of shortbread. "Invite them to a drinkies."

"Looks like Christmas has come early for someone!" said Tom, giving his brother a smile.

"Well, I'm due to drop Molly in for a service" he said, dusting off the crumbs as he stood up. "See you later".

They waved him on his way and got down to day-to-day matters. There was a surgery tomorrow when Tom's constituents could come along and talk to him about their problems with bureaucracy. He held these weekly meetings in a different part of the constituency so that people didn't feel left out if they lived in a particular area.

Tom poured himself another cup of coffee as they began to look through who was on the list and what their complaint was. It was a good way for a sitting MP to reconnect with real people and leave the Westminster bubble behind.

They both heard a loud bang which made the windows rattle, followed by a cacophony of car and building alarms going off.

They looked at each other for a moment, and Tom felt as if his blood had turned to ice.

"*Mike!*"

25

They scrambled downstairs. They could see a pall of smoke coming from Market Street which is the way Mike would have driven towards the garage to get Molly serviced.

People were coming out into the square to see what had happened. There was a subdued hush as people began to understand that this had not been a car backfiring.

Tom's mind was racing as he ran as fast as he could, leaving Muriel behind. He could see thick smoke and was aware of several cars that had been damaged by the blast. He smelt something he remembered from the Balkans, the residue from a home-made bomb. He thought he saw Mike through the smoke but kept running.

"Bruv!"

It was Mike looking shaken but unhurt. Tom couldn't quite understand what was happening. Others were milling around and the sound of a fire engine from the nearby fire station began to drown out his thoughts.

"I'm alright, Tom!" said Mike, reading his brother's incomprehension. "So is Molly" he added.

The Land Rover was in the middle of the road where Mike

had left it. There was a black scorch mark and a small crater in the middle of the road. Something was smouldering giving off acrid smoke. Tom guessed that it was the residue of the explosive burning.

"Looks like someone tried to stick a bomb under the wagon" said Mike matter-of-factly as Tom came to the same conclusion.

"I couldn't avoid that pothole" he said, pointing at another hole in the road. "Must've shaken it off!"

Tom finally realized what had happened. Somehow someone had attached an explosive device to Molly; Mike had been very lucky.

"You okay, Mike?" he said almost apologetically. This was the second occasion when he had almost died driving Tom around the constituency.

"Bit shaky, to be fair" Mike replied. Tom could see his face was pale.

"My ears are ringing" he added. Tom told him that the noise was all of the alarms going off, at which they both laughed and hugged each other.

At that moment a firefighter appeared with a large extinguisher and they were lost in a cloud of something to put out the fire. As they emerged from the smoke people recognised Tom and asked if he was alright, and what state his Land Rover was in.

"Tom! Mike! Thank God!" It was Muriel who had managed to get through the throng. The smoke was clearing and it looked like the damage was quite localised.

A uniformed police officer appeared, who also recognised Tom.

"Alright, Mr Scobie?" he said, relieved that he was not dealing with any fatalities. "Best leave everything as it is until we can get the bomb squad here to have a look."

"Any chance of another one of those shortbread fingers, Mu?" asked Mike.

* * *

Back in the office Tom's first thought was to call Anna and tell her that he was OK. As always, the sound of her voice was reassuring. He explained gently that there had been an unsuccessful attempt to blow up the Land Rover, but that he wasn't near it.

"What about poor Mike? He must think he's doomed if he keeps driving you around!" They both laughed, glad to hear each other. "Make sure that Mike gets looked over, he may have shock" she added. "And, well, look after yourself, Tom."

He looked at Muriel as she fussed over Mike with another mug of coffee and a plate of shortbread fingers.

"Back as soon as I can get a lift" he said, explaining that Molly was inside a police cordon.

The office phones began to ring, bringing them all back to the reality of what had just happened. Muriel took the first call and started to explain that Mr Scobie was unhurt as was his brother. She looked over at Tom; he was again thankful that Mu had agreed to remain as the mainstay of the constituency office. People knew her and trusted her, and this was the sort of time when her wisdom would be needed.

"That was the vicar!" she said.

"Hope he's not too disappointed not to be taking any funerals" said Mike, as he reached for another biscuit. They all laughed. Tom enjoyed the release of tension that gave them. Tom's phone peeped, it was DI Izzy Bannister.

"How did that happen?" She sounded rather cross that Tom had allowed his guard to drop.

"Well, I wasn't due to be here" he began as if explaining himself to a reproachful schoolteacher.

"Mike picked me up this morning and dropped me down at the office and was on his way to get a service for the Land Rover. It wasn't parked in a remote place and left unattended, at least not for long."

"Hmmm." Izzy sounded more emollient. "I'll get John Moran to come over and take some statements. Somebody must have seen something."

No sooner had Tom ended the call than his phone peeped again. This time it was Georgina. It sounded as if she was walking around somewhere.

"Tom! You alright? I heard there was an explosion in Wandage and imagined the worst"

"Bad news travels fast!" he said. He repeated his story, that he wasn't due to be in the constituency today, so it must have been an opportunistic attempt.

"You sound very calm; how is Anna?" she asked. "She must be getting fed up with this."

Tom knew that Georgina was still mourning the loss of her colleague Jack who had been able to uncover the Markham network. She had become very protective of him and Anna.

"Georgie, thank you for your kind thoughts." He didn't want to dismiss her concerns. "Anna is, well, she's got this inner steel that always amazes me. She's more concerned that my lovely brother is fine and well!"

They both laughed.

"I may get Dr Macdonald to give him the once-over" he continued. Mike looked to be unaffected by the event, but Anna would be able to spot any signs of a reaction.

"Just now I need a lift as my Land Rover is being examined" he added.

"Stay right there, I'm coming over for an interview." They ended the call.

Muriel answered another phone call, as Tom walked over to

the coffee pot for a refill. As he passed the second phone it rang, he picked it up and answered.

"You were lucky, Scobie. Next time...."

The phone went dead.

26

"Been in the wars, Scobie?" A rather pompous voice boomed through the Strangers' bar on the following Monday evening.

The Strangers' bar was another wood-panelled room that overlooked the river and gave on to a terrace where MPs and their guests gathered when the weather was clement.

The news was full of the 'assassination attempt in sleepy Oxfordshire market town', which had brought Wandage and the Vale of the White Horse its five minutes of fame. Locals had been stopped in the street and vox-popped by the media.

Tom was gratified to see that most of those interviewed thought he was a good bloke. For the sake of balance there was one person who worried that explosions going off in the town wasn't good for property prices.

"Sourpuss!" Anna had said when she saw the interview.

Tom had told DS Moran about the telephone call but they agreed there would be no chance to trace it. Tom didn't immediately recognise the voice but he would if he heard it again.

The bomb squad reported that the detonator had gone off but wasn't properly inserted into the plastic explosive. A small chunk of the explosive had detonated but the rest had just burned. Mike had collected Molly and driven it to the garage for its overdue service.

Tom wondered to himself whether this was intended as a warning, or if it was a rushed job. It seemed like a small charge from what he understood from the bomb squad's explanation.

Tom's parliamentary colleagues had offered to buy him a drink to congratulate him on his good fortune and - as one wag observed - to celebrate that they didn't have to troop down to the Ridgeway constituency to campaign for a bye-election.

"Nice to know you're appreciated!" he said as he sipped a glass of whisky. But as he joshed with his colleagues he knew that someone wanted to kill him. He had asked Sid to be more attentive to Anna and Naomi in Shepherds Cottage and got an earful for allowing his guard to drop.

"After everything," said Sid. "Bad dog – no biscuits!"

Tom smiled as he recalled the occasion when they had to navigate their way past some nasty guard dogs in the Balkans.

"What are you going to do about that toerag in the press gallery, Tom?" asked another colleague, bringing him back to the present.

"I've sent him a note inviting him for a sit-down" he replied.

"Sounds ominous!" someone said.

The division bell started clanging to end their bonhomie for the present.

"What are we voting on?" asked one as they headed out of the door towards the members' lobby.

"Dunno" came a reply. "The whips will tell us."

As he strolled with them towards the voting lobbies Tom reflected on the week ahead, meetings and committee meetings. Plus, he knew he had to have a further conversation with Adam from the security service to consider the next move regarding Toddy.

He had to work out how to get Don out of Northern Cyprus and lured somewhere that would enable an arrest.

He was still worried that Toddy might be duped into signing away his property rights having only recently got his family land back from the Bulgarian government. Not only was it prime real estate but the resort being planned would incorporate a casino, which would be a magnet for dodgy money. Toddy seemed to be entranced by the prospect of riches but blind to the risk he was running.

And there was Anna. She seemed content with the regime she was undergoing with Naomi to keep her calm and in good spirits as they got closer to her due date. He had to trust that Sid and Mike could keep them both safe until mini-Scobie made an appearance.

"Just another day at the office" someone said.

"Come on in, guys!" said Toddy as he welcomed the visitors to his house. "Mi casa su casa" he added, slapping Don on the back as he walked into the hallway. Don gave him a weak smile – could well be the case soon, he was thinking to himself.

Don had been contacted by Darren who suggested that it was time to move things along with their Varna project. His associates were getting impatient. It didn't take much persuading to set up the meeting the following day. Along with Don and Darren were two characters who Darren introduced as Dmitry and Ruslan.

Toddy waved them all through to his large sitting room where Tanya was pouring out glasses of champagne. She passed the tray of drinks to them all with a fixed smile on her face. As she did so, she made a face of disapproval at Toddy as he took his glass. He gave her a wink in return and took his glass.

"*Nazdrovie!*" he said, offering a toast. "To our success!"

Ruslan had a cardboard tube in his free hand. He put his glass down and pulled out what looked like an architect's drawing. Dmitry moved to help him, putting some ornaments on each corner to keep the paper flat.

"Our project" he said matter-of-factly while looking at Toddy.

This was the first time that Toddy had seen detailed drawings of how the new resort would look. He allowed himself time to examine the plans. He ran his finger over the paper as he sought to orient his point of view. The glossy sales brochure had artist's impressions of the new resort. These drawings were scaled and showed different elevations of the buildings.

"Like what you see?" asked Don. He was watching Toddy's reaction and thought he saw a distinct lack of enthusiasm.

"Looks promising" said Toddy, taking a sip from his glass. "Maybe there might be a model of some sort?"

Don wondered if Toddy was stalling for some reason. He would need to reassure him to keep the Russians on board. "That would be the next stage, Toddy" he said. "Like lots of projects these things go in phases." He was looking for a reaction. He was gratified to see Toddy nodding his understanding.

"So when I can look at a model I will be able to really understand how this will look" said Toddy, giving Don a blank look.

Don needed to regain control of the situation quickly or he would lose face in front of Darren and his Russian associates. A telephone rang in another room and they heard Tanya's footsteps as he answered the call.

There was a knock on the door and she opened it and beckoned to Toddy. He made a face at the group; Don made a gesture to signify that they would wait for him to take the call.

Dmitry beckoned Darren over to join him and Ruslan. As they huddled together Don felt a chill go down his spine. The old superstitious phrase of someone walking over his grave came to mind.

Darren broke away from the others and walked back towards Don; he took him by the arm and led him towards the table where the plan was lying. He tapped the paper and turned towards Don.

"They want this signed now, or they walk" he said.

27

Georgina looked around her. This was the first time she had been into Portcullis House, the building adjacent to the Palace of Westminster where many MPs had their offices.

"Very nice!" she said as she took a drink of coffee.

"We are humble servants of the people, so we need adequate space to do our work" replied Tom as he poured himself a cup.

Tom had asked Georgina to come into his office as he felt that matters were moving more quickly and he had got a full programme of events in the constituency blocked out for the weekend. There was no time to waste, he had told her.

"We need to move things along, Georgie" he said as he closed the door between his office and that of Amy and her colleague.

"Toddy has agreed to a grand signing ceremony to mark his deal with Don and the Russians and has asked me to be at the ceremony." He saw the alarm on her face.

"Has he agreed?" she asked.

"He managed a bit of *Vranyo*!" he said. "He said that he was willing to sign but why not make a big deal of it?" Georgina understood the concept of a Slavic form of double bluff.

Toddy had called Tom after his meeting with Don and the others. Their appearance and the sense of urgency had persuaded him that what Tom had told him about the people he was dealing was really true.

"Just hope it doesn't blow up in his face," said Georgina. "Have we got any leverage on Don, to pull him in?" she asked.

"I think we have to exercise a little *Vranyo* of our own" he replied. "Thanks to your colleague we've now got enough information about his little nest egg to go for a dangle…"

"A what?" asked Georgina, not quite sure what Tom meant.

"We can persuade him that we have the means to remove his stash of cash if he doesn't co-operate. He'll be left with nothing and probably be arrested as an accessory to some of Markham's crimes."

He explained that the plan was to persuade Don to reveal what he knew about Markham's network; in return he would be placed in a witness protection programme, as he would have to betray some big names including Markham, who might be able to find him and kill him.

He went on to say that if Toddy was co-operative, which he now seemed to be, he would not be prosecuted by the UK government and should emerge with an enhanced status which would do his political prospects no harm.

She nodded her understanding as he continued.

"DI Bannister says that they could try for an extradition of Don with our Bulgarian friends as a test of their belief in the rule of law."

"Really?" She made a face. "I'm sure they'd have a lawyer, not to say a judge in their pocket."

Tom nodded his agreement. The idea that Darren and his Russian friends would come meekly was something they'd have to work on; but Darren was a UK national so he could hopefully be swept up in the same net.

"In which case we need a plan B" he said. He saw Georgina's puzzled expression. "Let's say a contingency plan just to make sure."

"Will that help Toddy?" she asked.

He paused. "I'm going to have to do some fast talking on the day" he said, "but I think he'll go along with what I'm thinking."

* * *

Don allowed his mind to wander as he closed his eyes. It had been a fraught few days but he felt that he had managed to persuade Toddy that the proposed deal with Darren and the Russians was worth backing. They both needed each other, he reasoned.

Toddy wanted a big deal to cement his place in Bulgarian society and win a place in Parliament whereas a legislator he'd be immune from prosecution. Darren and his associates wanted somewhere to place their investments. Plus, the plan for the casino meant that there would be enough liquidity to launder the proceeds of their other investments.

He would get the credit for that, but he had to land the deal with Toddy. There was a moment when he thought he'd lost the whole deal, but Toddy had come through. There was something still in the back of his mind that nagged at him. Why had he got the impression that Toddy was having second thoughts?

The fly in the ointment was Tom Scobie. A weak link which neither he nor the Russians liked. Once Darren had explained the situation, they had all approved of Toddy inviting Tom to the signing. As Ruslan had said, there was plenty of concrete he could get hold of if necessary.

He allowed himself a smile as he listened to the cool breeze and the shushing sound of the waves on the shore. Definitely getting cooler, he thought.

"Good afternoon again" came a familiar voice.

Don opened his eyes to see the smiling figure of Father Peter standing in front of him. He needed to sharpen up and not to allow his guard to drop.

"May I join you?" said Father Peter as he pulled up a chair. Don was by now fully awake and able to be civil to his visitor. Once again, his guest was pleased to accept a cup of coffee.

"So nice to see you again, Don, I enjoyed our talk." He was carrying a small brown paper package. He reached across and placed it in front of Don. It looked like a small thin book.

"It is an icon" he explained, as Don picked up the package and turned it over and over in his hands.

Don carefully unwrapped the package. A small piece of wood emerged as he pulled open the paper.

"It is Saint John of Rila – I believe that you have been in Bulgaria?"

That got Don's attention. This nice old boy was not as dozy as he thought. He sat up and took a sip of his drink.

"Tell me more!" said Don, deciding to explore where this conversation might go. His instinct told him that this chap was not going to hurt him and might have some information that could be useful to him.

"My brothers and I want good things for you, Don. We don't want you to fall into the hands of bad people who tell you that they are your friends." He paused, waiting to see how Don reacted.

"We have been able to build bridges between people, some who have ancient hatred going back through the ages." He made a gesture with his right hand as if throwing something away.

"Sometimes it is good to start with a clean page. None of us is perfect" he continued, "we are all a work in progress."

Don's mind was struggling to understand what he was hearing but he caught the echo of an idea from somewhere.

"Are you speaking of *forgiveness?*" he asked. He saw the face of Father Peter change into a warm smile as he nodded silently.

"I too have been where you are now" he said. That caught Don's attention. What did this man know about him, and who had told him.

"Oh?" He tried not to sound too hostile, but he needed to understand where this was going. He looked around for anybody lurking in the shadows waiting to grab him. No-one. Nothing.

"A long time ago I learnt a very difficult lesson, but I am here now" he said.

This was a very different topic of conversation from the one he had been having with Darren and the Russians. They were about shaking down Toddy with a dodgy deal and killing Tom Scobie. It all made sense at the time.

"I see you are troubled about which path to follow," said Father Peter. "Look on the back of the icon" he said in a kindly voice.

Don turned over the small piece of wood and looked at what had been painted with a fine brush onto the back.

'*1 Timothy 6:10*'

Father Peter saw the puzzled look on Don's face.

"For the love of money is the root of all evil" he said in the same kindly voice. "I don't judge, Don; I want you to choose the right path."

Don nodded, as he recalled the last time they had met and the scripture verse about life and death. He was beginning to formulate a reply that he hoped would encourage Father Peter that he would like to find a way out of the maze he found himself in. He was brought up short by what the priest said next.

"The Proton account is not safe," said Father Peter.

Don's blood ran cold. This man knew. If he knew, who else knew? It was Markham's idea to name the bank fund the Proton account, something to do with building blocks. Don knew that a bank in Zurich was the ultimate storage facility, but the route there was via cut-out accounts in Northern Cyprus and Bermuda.

"You're not a poker player, Don" said Father Peter in what sounded like a disappointed voice. "Even if I was bluffing your face gives you away."

Don was still trying to process what he had just learnt. What was all this talk of forgiveness? Was this man suggesting some sort of deal? He needed to say something – anything to regain control of the situation.

"Are you some sort of go-between?" he asked. "An inter-mediary?"

Father Peter nodded. "I want to help you Don, not punish you; but maybe you have to decide which side you are on."

A hint of a smile crossed Don's lips. He saw that Father Peter noticed this. Maybe there is a way to come out of this with a smile on my face, he thought.

28

"Are you messing with his head?" Anna asked as they drove to a constituency event on the following Sunday. She had brushed up for this occasion, wearing a long skirt in her family tartan and a loose-fitting moss-green jacket that set off her copper-coloured hair.

Tom had brought her up-to-date as they drove together. Cousin Naomi had gone away for the weekend and he didn't like to divulge too much when she was around.

"Don is definitely the weak link in this case" he continued. "He is venal and greedy. Markham is nasty and corrupt. Markham managed to ensnare him with the promise of lots of money. Since he went inside, Don has been the custodian. If Markham thought that he would rat on him he'd have him killed."

"Honour among thieves!" said Anna. She was a shrewd judge of character, and Tom was often grateful for her level-headed reading of some of the nasty things he discussed with her.

"I'm still amazed that Markham can control people from prison" she said.

"I've got an idea about that" he said.

Anna held up both of her hands. "Can we enjoy this lunch without talking about him?"

Tom nodded. He understood her frustration that they were still dealing with the fall-out of the election campaign and Markham's attempt to steal it.

They arrived at the venue for the Sunday lunchtime event. Muriel had persuaded one of her wide circle of friends to be a guest speaker. She was a celebrity who appeared on daytime TV. Tom was definitely the warm-up act, which suited him fine.

As they entered the fine Cotswold style farmhouse there were lots of smiles and handshakes. Tom was congratulated on his good fortune at avoiding the recent car bomb attempt, which seemed to have faded in people's minds. There was a lot of fussing over Anna and her bump, which they had christened mini-Scobie.

"Have you heard the news?" was the first question Muriel asked as he saw her. "Wyvern Hall is up for sale. Looks like Lady M is off!"

Wyvern Hall had been Markham's residence where he used to host extravagant parties, to win friends and influence people. Or intimidate them.

"Perhaps our guest might like to buy it" Tom suggested as he took a glass of champagne from a passing tray.

"She's actually going from here to do a viewing!" Muriel said with obvious delight. "Come and say hello." She led him over towards the guest speaker who was dressed in classic country casual style with just the right amount of jewellery.

"Sooo pleased to meet you, Tim, what a lovely occasion!" she gushed. He didn't bother to correct her, as he shook hands and suggested that he should mingle. She gave him her TV smile and turned to another guest.

He caught up with Anna who was among a group of people

chatting to the owner of the house, a prosperous estate agent who was the one selling Wyvern Hall.

"Couldn't believe my luck" he was saying as Tom joined the group. "Mary called and said 'I'm selling William, can you give me a valuation?' - just like that."

He made sure that Anna was comfortable and got a nod and a smile from her in acknowledgement. It was good to see that big wide smile again. He shook hands briefly with the host and after a quick word of thanks for the hospitality he broke away and started to work his way around the room.

There was a lot of talk about how the new coalition government was working: some in favour, others against. He explained that he was in listening mode which enabled him to avoid having to explain areas of party policy he was unsure of.

As the conversation ebbed and flowed he thought he heard a familiar voice amidst the hubbub. As a young boy his grandfather had taken him into the woods to listen for different birdsongs. As a result, he could discern differences in the modulation of voices, a useful skill in crowded rooms like this.

He nodded as someone was speaking about agricultural policies, a subject he was familiar with. But he was trying to pick out the voice he thought he had heard on the phone. He said that he would have a word with his colleague in the agricultural ministry at the earliest opportunity and took the chance to move on.

In his mind's eye he was trying to recall the character he had met at a similar event, who had said something about being lucky. Maybe his mistake was to use the same formula of words. Tom decided to step outside and take a look at some of the cars parked in the field next to the house, in the hope of recognising the car he'd driven off in.

"Alright, Tom?" he turned and saw Jane, one of the ward chairmen. "Just doing a bit of car spotting!" he replied.

"Heard about what happened" she continued. "D'you need a new car? My hubby could sort you out". He remembered that her husband and Henry Makepeace were petrol-heads. Her husband John was in the car business.

As they walked together they chatted about life in Westminster and goings on locally. "You've heard about Wyvern Hall?" she said. "Sounds as if her ladyship is cashing in her chips and leaving."

"And here we are!" said Tom. He'd found a close approximation to the car he'd seen previously.

"Ah! Thought so!" Jane had walked around the car and spotted something on the rear numberplate. The name of her husband's garage.

"Would you be able to find out who owns this?" he asked.

"Well...." she said sheepishly, tapping the side of her nose.

As they walked back into the house she made a call to her husband and asked if he could find out who bought the car.

On entering the house Jane went off to hang up her coat, while Tom grabbed another glass and wandered into the room where the guest of honour was just about to begin. The host waved at Tom, encouraging him to say a few introductory words.

He kept his remarks short, thanking everybody for supporting this event and their gracious hosts. As he was speaking he was able to scan the crowd. He saw a familiar-looking profile at the back of the room. This time there was no convenient French window for him to leave by. Once he'd brought the guest of honour onto the stage, he stepped away and walked to the side of the room. He saw Anna wave at him from a chair that had been set to the side close to where the speaker stood.

The guest of honour didn't disappoint as she revealed what really went on behind the scenes of daytime TV. The audience was captivated as she dropped famous names into her speech.

Tom sidled around the edge of the room to get a better look at his quarry. He was pretty certain that it was the same man.

What to do? He couldn't make a scene, but he wanted to understand who the link to Markham was. Out of the corner of his eye he saw Jane moving equally carefully towards him. She had a piece of paper in her hand. Standing next to him she slid the paper towards him which he took. Glancing down he saw a name.

"Gotcha!" he muttered to himself.

* * *

"Knowledge is power," said Georgina. Tom had called her as he drove back to Shepherds Cottage. She said that she would double check via her own sources on whether Jane's information tallied with what was available through open sources. They hadn't succeeded last time but she was determined to get it right this time.

"DVLA and the electoral roll plus Land Registry." She reeled off the agencies she would approach. "Got my own sources" she added enigmatically.

"Doesn't she ever sleep?" asked Anna after he'd finished the call.

"This is personal," said Tom. "Anything she can do to lay the ghost of Jack..."

"Uh huh" she said. "I just hope she can find some sort of peace after all this is over" she said looking out at the autumnal landscape.

"How much longer, Tom?" she said. "This is...." They both kept silent. Tom knew that Anna was choosing her words carefully and he didn't want to cut her off.

"I'd like to think that our child won't have to get used to this"

she said. "You're doing the right thing, I know you are, but sometimes I just wonder...." She broke off.

"I hope so too" he said gently. "I hope that we can all enjoy a
family Christmas and look forward to a happy new year."

They continued in silence. He needed to finish this business.
Anna had been supportive of his efforts to put right what
Markham had been doing, but he hadn't foreseen that it would
drag on because Markham was still able to pull strings from
behind bars.

"Time to finish it", he said to himself.

29

"Remember Tom, this is about elicitation not pinning him to the wall" Matt's voice echoed in his mind as he walked into the wine bar close to Embankment tube station.

Both he and Matt knew about having tricky conversations with dodgy people from their earlier lives. Tom wanted to check with Matt how he thought he should handle this occasion.

He had sent a note via the internal post to Gordon, suggesting there were matters of mutual interest that they might usefully discuss. Surprisingly the response had been quite swift and they agreed to meet away from Parliament.

Tom was feeling tense as he went to the meeting. A lot was riding on this encounter. He had to get Gordon to believe that the money supply from Markham, via the Proton account, had dried up. A case of *Vranyo,* which he hoped that the journalist would swallow.

He saw that Gordon was already installed in a corner table so that he could look out into the room. Clever, thought Tom. He was wearing his characteristically flamboyant clothing, a loud checked jacket with mustard corduroy trousers. No danger that their encounter would be discreet thought Tom. Gordon rose in his seat as Tom approached and waved him to join him with a smile which wasn't echoed by his eyes. Tom reciprocated with an equally false smile as he sat down.

"Wine?" said Gordon, trying to take control of the conversation.

"Thank you" Tom replied. He'd let Gordon start talking and see where things went.

"Good of you to find the time to join me," said Gordon. It had been Tom's suggestion, but he let it pass. He chose a glass of red and they both began to look at the menu.

"Light business today, so I think we're safe from any votes interrupting us" said Tom, signifying that he wasn't in a hurry. They ordered their lunch along with some more wine. As this was Tom's invitation he would be paying.

"How do you feel things are going? I hear that there is disquiet in the Party" said Gordon fishing for some gossip. A slight variation from their last encounter. Tom took a sip of his wine whilst he considered his answer.

"It's no secret that some people have had to be passed over for ministerial posts" Tom began. "I can understand their disappointment, but the PM has bound our new partners into the coalition, so he has secured a payroll vote with them all voting to support the programme of legislation."

This was hardly premium gossip but Gordon nodded and smiled as he spoke. Perhaps he was hoping for some indiscretions as the wine flowed. As the food was served, they reverted to mundane chit chat about various characters in the government, some of whom Tom had to admit he had never met, not being a career politician.

"So, Tom" said Gordon "how can we help each other?" Time for some *Vranyo,* thought Tom.

"Markham manages to retain control of his network even while he's behind bars" began Tom.

Gordon nodded as this was a known fact. No revelations so far, he thought.

"My ambition is to ensure that his network gets wrapped up and some of his accomplices, shall we say facilitators share his fate," said Tom. He saw that this remark had caught Gordon's attention.

"How would you achieve that?"

"Well, I can use parliamentary privilege to call attention to them, then allow the police and judicial authorities to do the rest" he went on. Now he had definitely got Gordon's attention.

"And can I assist in this process?" Gordon asked guilelessly. He was surprised to see Tom nodding as he took another sip of wine.

"You can stop peddling falsehoods about me for a start" Tom began. "Because it won't do you any good, now that we have managed to turn off the money supply. You won't get paid for planting false stories, and once people realise you're a sham they won't speak to you. You'll probably lose your lobby accreditation." He could see Gordon's reaction as the series of assertions registered.

"The money supply?" he asked.

"You've been paid by Markham's account to spread rumours about his enemies over the years, and now the good times have come to an end. My friends, who are also journalists, have unearthed his accounts and they're in the process of being frozen."

Gordon's face was commendably blank. He probably thought Tom was bluffing so he had to reveal a little more. "One of my constituents, Andy Swift, has been managing Markham's accounts and now he won't be doing it anymore" said Tom. The mention of the name had registered with Gordon, and Tom had noticed. And Gordon had seen that he had.

"You know that the Speaker took notice of what Kathleen

Quinlan has said in her complaint, you don't want another one now do you." Tom pressed home his advantage.

Gordon continued to pick at his food as Tom spoke. He knew that MPs could use parliamentary privilege to raise matters in the chamber. Now that proceedings were broadcast live there was nothing he could do once the genie was out of the bottle. The Speaker might rule him out of order, but he would then have to sue Tom for libel which would prolong the things. Or he could do nothing, in which case the matter would have been proven by his inability to pursue Tom legally.

"How did you trace the money?" he asked.

"Perhaps I should protect my sources," said Tom. "You as a journalist will understand that".

He had to hope that Gordon had swallowed his story and would turn off his toxic tap.

* * *

Georgina and Matt had never actually met although they knew about each other. Tom had arranged for them both to come to supper at Shepherds Cottage the following Friday evening. Naomi was also there so it was a merry gang that set to in the kitchen to get supper going whilst Anna supervised.

"Are you some sort of undercover vicar, Matt?" asked Naomi as she began to understand how he fitted into Tom's world.

"I work in something called reconciliation ministry" he said, "and also in what we term restorative justice." He saw a blank look on her face.

"You might say that we folk of the cloth can go where others can't" he continued. "We can build bridges and sometimes we can help to put things right through our good offices." Matt in turn looked at Georgina who was pulling plates out of a cupboard under Anna's supervision. "Plus we have a worldwide network" he added as he found a corkscrew.

Tom had told both Georgina and Matt to be cautious about what they said in front of Naomi, not because he didn't trust her but just in case she said something to somebody who knew somebody. They understood, but there was a need for them all to gather and consider the next move.

"So how do we find the pot of gold?" asked Georgina. Having identified the Proton account the next step was to be able to access it, or to enable the funds to be removed so that Markham could no longer use them to operate his network of influence.

"My associates think we've found someone who wants to redeem themselves." Matt began speaking obliquely although Naomi was now consulting with Anna over the preparation of supper.

"A lot of corrupt or criminal activity is carried out by people who have got wrapped up in something and then found that they are in too deep to get out. We can offer them a way out by talking to local law enforcement people and arranging a plea bargain."

"It's all about people," said Tom. "A lot of things come down to individuals taking decisions. We need to help them make the right ones."

"Sounds simple enough" said Georgina "but I know that Jack got caught up in this stuff and...." She looked away.

The sound of a cork popping lightened the atmosphere.

"How was Gordon the lobby hack?" asked Matt as he poured out glasses of wine. Anna was drinking something Tom called an evil brew but which was in fact a cordial.

"I hope he bought the story" he said as he raised a glass.

"One down, one to go"

30

"As certain as I can be" said Georgina when she had confirmed the identity of the mystery man who had been at the lunch party. Now they knew who was handling the money from the UK side, they now needed to turn off the tap to Markham and his cronies.

After the council of war at Shepherds Cottage Tom had then checked with Muriel to confirm that the money man was a paid-up member of the Party.

"Regular as clockwork" came the reply. "His standing order comes in promptly." His name was not on the list of 'Bandits' that her husband had compiled when he had been the chairman of the constituency association.

He worked for a well-known high street clearing bank, which would enable him to manage transactions in a way that didn't attract undue attention.

"Also Tom, I found out something else." Muriel sounded as if she was teasing him. "He's a registered prison visitor."

"Well, well, a real upstanding citizen!" he said. "I think I might just pay a house call."

Muriel cautioned him to be careful, as this chap had

managed to remain hidden in plain sight whilst the Markham network appeared to collapse. He might have some nasty connections who could emerge from the woodwork if needed.

"I'm just going to drop off some raffle tickets" he said jovially. "I'm not going to cause a scene, I know he has young children at home so I'll be Mister Geniality!" he added.

"I just need to deliver a message".

He had busied himself around the constituency. After the failed bomb attack Tom had been to see Mike and his wife to reassure her that what happened was something that would hopefully never occur again, if they succeeded in pulling down Markham's support network.

"I just worry that lightning managed to strike twice" his wife had said. "I'm not so sure that you'll both be so lucky a third time."

Tom was able to tell her that his old friend Sid had given Mike some top tips on how to spot nasty things that shouldn't be attached to the Land Rover, and she appeared to be mollified.

Mike was restored to driving duty, so early in the evening he drove Tom to the address of Andy Swift the money man and pulled up at the end of his driveway.

"Won't be long" Tom said over his shoulder as he walked down the path towards the neat bungalow. As well as an expensive-looking car parked in the driveway he could hear the sound of a TV programme, so it looked like everybody was at home.

He knocked on the door and waited. He held a book of raffle tickets in his hand which he flicked to fan the pages. He hoped this would present a relaxed image. The door was opened by what looked like a child of nine or ten.

"Evening, young Sir" said Tom with what he hoped was his widest smile. "Daddy home?" he asked.

"Dad...." called the youngster who stepped away as an adult came along the hallway.

"Evening!" beamed Tom. "It's that time of year again, so I thought you'd like to be one of the first to get your hands on our raffle tickets!" As he said this he pushed the book of raffle tickets into the hands of the surprised person standing in his doorway.

"Er – great, thanks, Tom" he managed to say but Tom could see the alarm in his face.

"Lots of good prizes this year" continued Tom "so your friends and neighbours will want to snap them up" he beamed.

"Yes, of course." He was beginning to recover his poise. "Very good of you to drop them off in person...."

Tom made to turn away. "Of course, you could buy the whole lot. That way you'd stand a better chance of winning" he added.

"Ah! Yes, I suppose so."

"You only need to be lucky once" said Tom as he waved and turned down the pathway.

* * *

"This is beginning to smell bad," said Darren. He had come to talk to Don about the worries of his Russian business partners. They were sitting in Don's usual beachfront taverna.

"My friends have told me that unless something changes, and quickly, the deal's off".

This brought Don up short. He thought that the Russians were committed to the Varna project and that he could move things along and get round whatever obstacles lay in their path.

"Why the change of heart?" he asked. He needed to understand what had changed. Was it that they were getting impatient? Well, he could give Toddy some encouragement to sign the contract that they needed.

"They have got wind that Scobie is getting close to the source of *your* money and they don't like leaky projects" said Darren. The tone of his voice was conversational but the message was concerning. The Russians saw him as part of the problem.

"It's in my interest to see that this project works" said Don, needing to persuade Darren that he at least was committed to the project.

"Toddy will do the right thing" he added as he poured himself another glass. He offered the bottle to Darren who accepted the offer. As he poured another glass, he was reassured, as it meant that Darren hadn't just come to deliver a message and leave.

"Let's talk it through" he continued, taking a sip.

"The weak link is Scobie," said Darren. "He is mates with Toddy, and we know that he has been in touch with him." Don nodded at this, no surprise there.

"Scobie has been on the trail of your old boss, and now he's onto you, Don"

That same conversational tone contained an element of menace. Don thought of himself as a survivor, so now he began to move into survival mode.

"I got to know Scobie while I was his constituency agent" Don began. "He's a boy scout who has got out of his depth" he added. He hoped that this insight would be reassuring.

"He ran rings around your boss and seems to have wrapped up his whole business, I don't think that's scouting for boys," said Darren.

"He got lucky" replied Don, knowing that it was a lame riposte but it was the best he could do on the spur of the moment.

"Scobie is coming to celebrate the signature of the Varna deal," said Don. "That's an opportunity...." He left the thought hanging in the air.

Darren made a face as if he'd just smelt something unpleasant.

"I think that will have to be down to you, Don" he said coolly.

* * *

"So we can get a flight to Zurich and doorstep this person?" said Georgina. "We'd better move fast, once our friends know what we're up to they might get there ahead of us" she added with a tone of urgency in her voice.

"Do you know something I don't know" asked Tom who was pouring himself a cup of coffee in the skunk works where Georgina's operation was based.

"Perhaps I've got a sixth sense about this" she added. "They have always seemed to be one step ahead of us".

Tom nodded as he came back to the table which was once again spread with pieces of paper and a laptop. It was late on a Thursday evening and he was on his way back home. Georgina had suggested that he stopped by en route.

"My brother is an architect" she continued. "The other day he was talking to me about a tricky bit of work he is doing that involves a single load-bearing joint".

Tom nodded to encourage her to continue with her train of thought. He had often relied on Anna's sixth sense about people and situations, so he was open minded. "My blood ran cold as he was speaking" she continued. "He thought I was going to faint, but I said I was OK. But I realised that everything now hangs on this one individual. If we can persuade him to help us...."

Tom waved a finger in the air to slow her down.

"I need to speak to Matt about what conversations his colleagues have had with this person. What it was that they spoke about to unlock this possibility."

He knew that when he was speaking to people who wanted

to help him, when he was in the Balkans, there was often a complex pathway that needed to be trod. Their motivations could be anything from the petty, such as jealousy, to the high-minded.

"I understand, Georgie" he wanted to reassure her that he was not dragging his heels. "If someone gets wind of what we're thinking then we've lost our chance of wrapping this whole rotten business up."

31

"I'm excited about this, Don!" Toddy sounded as enthusiastic as ever as they spoke on the phone.

Don had called Toddy as soon as Darren had left him. He was still sitting at the beachfront taverna and had decided that there was no time like the present.

"I was just wondering, Toddy, our friends are also excited about the Varna project." He tried to match Toddy's gushing tone.

"Any chance that we could bring the signature date forward?"

There was a pause. Don held his breath.

"Why not!" came the response. Don allowed himself to breathe again.

"It's my birthday soon, why don't we use that as the chance to celebrate?"

"Ah ha!" said Don. They both agreed on a date.

The next small matter was to arrange for some 'friends' of Don's to be put on the invite list. He was going to have to find someone locally who could manage the Scobie problem. He recalled that Lord Markham had kept a list of people who could be useful in his little black book. He had made a copy one night while Markham was sleeping off another successful deal.

He settled the bill for the drinks and gave his favourite waiter the usual tip. He was in good spirits as he walked back to the apartment he rented overlooking the beach. This time there were no orthodox clergy in sight to harangue him about his moral duty. This was survival, morals would have to wait a little longer.

He had initially thought of his apartment as his hideaway but now he began to think of it as, what? A launch-pad perhaps.

He found the anonymous-looking cardboard box that he'd been able to grab when he left Wandage. Riffling through the memory sticks he found the one he wanted. He got his laptop going and put on some coffee whilst it powered up.

He checked his watch and noted the time difference between Cyprus and the UK. It would be early evening back home.

He found the name he wanted. It had a mobile phone number and an email address. No time like the present, he reminded himself as he took a swig of his coffee. He needed a clear head for this conversation.

He tapped the numbers into his phone. As expected, the phone went to voicemail. The recipient of the call would most likely be on a job somewhere and wouldn't want to be disturbed. He had formulated his message.

"Good evening, this is Don speaking. I believe we have a mutual acquaintance who is unavoidably detained" he began. The recipient wouldn't recognise his voice but he would understand who he was referring to - Markham.

"I have an interesting opportunity for you if you don't mind a bit of travel to do the job. It'll be worth your while, and it'll make our friend very happy."

* * *

Matt had agreed to meet Tom after he had called him. Tom explained Georgina's concern. They both had time on the Friday morning, so Tom offered to treat Matt to a brunch meeting at a nearby gastro inn.

"We know a lot of people in the finance world" Matt began. "They're the people who oil the wheels of big international deals so they travel a lot."

So far so good, thought Tom. They ordered their food and coffee and Matt returned to his story. At this hour there were empty tables close to them, so they felt free to talk.

"Some of them are big philanthropists and they give generously to charities and good causes. Others are also well-intentioned but don't have the big money that can change lives. But they know people who know people." This was familiar territory for both of them, as they had operated in the grey world between good and bad.

"Someone approached one of our colleagues and told them that they were troubled by some of the work they were being asked to do. They knew it was money-laundering but they were not in a position to do anything about it."

"A whistle-blower?" asked Tom.

Matt shook his head. They paused as the coffee arrived. They thanked the waiter and watched as he retraced his steps to the kitchen.

"This person is too junior to risk their career and income by blowing a whistle. Remember this is Switzerland; they'd never get another job and could get prosecuted for revealing confidential information."

Tom nodded as he recalled that Switzerland had draconian laws designed to enforce client confidentiality.

"So we wind up acting as a sort of conduit to preserve their identity" Matt added.

"Any chance that someone could discover their identity?" asked Tom.

Matt paused, which alarmed Tom. He had expected a straight response that all was well.

"I want to say not, but we both know that nothing is ever one hundred percent watertight. The probability that this source is safe is in the high ninety percent range, though" he added.

Their food arrived and they both tucked into the plates in front of them. "Georgie wants to get over to Zurich and meet this person as soon as possible" said Tom.

Matt nodded his understanding as he was eating.

"I need to contact my colleague and see if that would be agreeable" he said. "If you just want this person to empty the account, then the finger would point straight at our source. You need to think about what you're going to ask them to do that can be helpful."

That pulled Tom up short. He had hoped that they could simply remove the money to a safe place which would mean that Don would have nothing to offer the folks he was dealing with over the Varna project.

As Tom chewed on his food he realised that he and Georgina hadn't worked this move out. They needed to think before they did something that would not only be fruitless, but which would also risk exposing their source.

32

Markham enjoyed a game of chess. He enjoyed outwitting his opponents who were often preoccupied by the next move, whereas he was usually two or three moves ahead. So when his occasional visitor Andy came to visit with a tale about Tom turning up on his doorstep his antenna started twitching.

"He was right there on my doorstep!" Andy had said. Markham was annoyed at first, as he used these visits as an opportunity to send and receive messages to his associates on the outside.

But he allowed his thoughts to ponder what Scobie was up to. He had relied on his wits to build up his business empire. Somehow Scobie had managed to outwit him, but only because of a turncoat in his inner sanctum. He had underestimated Scobie, imagining him to be a rather dull farmer's boy who had dutifully served in an undistinguished infantry regiment.

"What did Scobie say to you exactly?" asked Markham. He needed to understand the context of the meeting between them.

"Nothing threatening you understand" Andy replied. "It was

just that he said, 'you only need to be lucky once' which was what I had been told to say to him."

Markham's network relied on different people doing specific things, but no one person could see the whole picture apart from him. Under the circumstances he had come to rely more on the efforts of Don Johnson to manage his network. Perhaps he had been careless. Ah well, no one is indispensable, he thought.

"Now then, Andy, listen to me" Markham began. "I need you to do the following....." Something made him pause. There was a new warder on duty not one he recognised. Markham gestured to the new warder and waved him over with a friendly smile.

"Don't think we've met" Markham began. The warder came over with a matching smile.

"Where's Stevie?" Markham continued in the same matey tone. "He's been suspended" came the reply. Markham maintained his pleasant smile, but even Andy could spot the change in his pallor.

"Anything you want me to be getting on with?" Andy asked as the warder passed on his way. He could see that Markham was trying to work out what Stevie's suspension might mean. The warder hadn't volunteered any additional information. In a prison knowledge was power, so he would have to trade something to get what he wanted. Back to the bigger picture, he needed to think about the next move and the one after that. First of all he needed Andy to pass a message to Don.

* * *

Once again Tom had taken himself for a walk around White Horse Hill, the place where he liked to do his thinking. He felt that the history of the place allowed him to connect to what he was going through. This place was thousands of years old and would still be there long after he was gone. It gave him a sense of perspective.

Normally he would walk with Anna, but Naomi who was fast becoming the auxiliary midwife ruled out a strenuous walk.

He needed to bring this matter to a close; it was eating up their lives. He was worried about Toddy and the risk of his being seduced by the very real prospect of some serious money once the Russians had opened their casino as part of the 'project' they were pushing.

He wanted to be able to bring in Don, and either persuade him to unveil the rest of Markham's network or face the prospect of a long jail sentence. His own bet was that Don would co-operate as he knew he probably wouldn't be safe in prison. Markham's cronies would find him.

The prospect of Toddy's birthday and the signature of an agreement in Varna was the opportunity to get all the fish in one net. It would be risky. Now Tom was about to be a father his appetite for some of the crazy stuff he did previously had lessened. He would need to get Sid involved somehow.

"Good afternoon, Tom!" A friendly voice broke into his thoughts. It was a couple out walking. He recognised the man as someone who had come to see him at one of his constituency surgeries.

"Thanks for your help with the school" he said.

"Let me know if there's anything we can do to help" Tom replied. He vaguely recalled something about Special Educational Needs and a child who had learning difficulties.

They carried on walking as Tom resumed his thinking. The Russian element was a complication. He'd need to speak to Adam and see what approach the security services might recommend.

The sky was looking overcast. He decided that it might be time to return to Shepherds Cottage. Naomi insisted that Anna build up her strength for the forthcoming birth and provided a decent spread at teatime. He felt sufficiently virtuous after walking up the hill to be able to enjoy the home-made brownies and tea, so started back.

33

"Another day, another dollar" said Tom as he and Muriel left the village hall where his weekly surgery had just finished.

"Hopefully we have some satisfied constituents?" said Muriel. She was asking how Tom felt the session had gone. She had been busy shepherding people in and out.

"All apart from the bloke who just came to moan about the new coalition, I think we can help. I never cease to wonder at the way the bureaucrats can gum up the works in what seems like common sense matters."

"I think all of the bureaucrats who used to run the empire have been reincarnated in our local council offices!" said Muriel.

They both laughed and Tom passed over his file of case notes to Muriel, as she walked off in the direction of her car. She waved over her shoulder as she went.

Tom let out a sigh of relief, that was his duty done for another week. Now he could think about Anna and her breathing exercises. He still couldn't quite believe that he was going to be a father. Cousin Matt had a saying: if you want to make God laugh, tell him what your plans are. Very true in this case.

Tom's sixth sense made him turn around as he heard the sound of footsteps behind him. Two figures were walking towards him purposefully. He recognised the Smurfit brothers.

"Wanna word with you, Scobie!" said Jed, whom he had last encountered in his ramshackle home. His companion looked like his brother who was handy with a knife.

Tom felt the adrenaline even as the brother flicked his knife open. Intended as an intimidation, it only confirmed Tom's intention to deal with him first. Jed looked like he enjoyed too many pies to start serious trouble.

Tom kept an eye on the blade of the knife whilst being aware that the brother was lunging towards him. Tom was able to be ambidextrous when needed, and this was one such occasion.

With his right arm he made as if to punch his assailant, who dodged to avoid it. Tom saw that the knife was held as if to stab not just to slash, so he needed to shift his weight to turn away from the downward lunge. Once committed his assailant was intent on following through with his weight behind the knife.

Tom was able to grab his wrist with his left hand and divert the effort into an uncomfortable armlock behind the back of his attacker. A shout of pain and frustration told Tom he'd managed to blunt the force of the attack.

He saw that Jed had decided to weigh in, so with his right hand he grabbed the belt of the knifeman and shifted both of them into the path of his brother, who was taking a swing at Tom. Instead, he wound up walloping his brother in the face.

He heard the smack of fist on the head of his attacker, who grunted again. Tom was able to twist the arm of the attacker so that he dropped the knife which Tom kicked away from them.

Jed came back for a second try, grunting with the effort he was having to make. Tom pushed the now disarmed knife-wielder away, who slumped down stunned. As Jed swung at him, he dodged under the punch and put his own weight behind a fine upper cut under Jed's jaw which sent him sprawling.

By now Muriel and several others had come to see what was going on. The Smurfit brothers were now confronted with a crowd who were laughing at their shambolic performance.

As they picked themselves up, Tom saw that neither of them had any fight left in them. Without the knife they had nothing to threaten Tom with; the people standing around would all be witness to anything they decided to do.

Tom allowed himself to relax. He could feel the adrenaline pulsing and he needed to regain control of himself. One of the bystanders had picked up the knife and handed it to Tom. He noted that it was a very sharp lock-knife. It could have been a very different story had he not sensed something was up. He folded the blade and put it into his pocket.

The assailants walked off the way they had come, elbowing past some of the crowd that had gathered. Tom gave them a wave, to signify that the show was over and that he was unharmed. He turned to re-join Muriel.

"How did they know where to find you?" was Muriel's first question. "By the way, are you okay?" she added. She had got used to Tom's scrapes by now.

"We advertise the weekly surgery on the website," said Tom. "I suppose someone could have told them."

"We only tell the people on the list where we're going to be, for security" she said.

"We should have a look at the list" he replied. "I'm suspicious of the bloke who came with nothing really to deal with, maybe he was in cahoots with them. And yes, I'm fine thanks for asking!" he said with a smile as he pretended to dust himself off.

"You goin' to call the coppers?" asked one of the bystanders, a lady with a shopping bag. Muriel went over to her and began writing down her phone number. She turned towards Tom and waved him away.

"Get home safely, Tom!" for once her habitual greeting had more meaning.

* * *

"Very nasty" said DS Moran. He had come up to Shepherds Cottage to take a statement from Tom. He was now holding the knife that had been used in the attack. He turned it over and activated the spring mechanism. The blade flicked open with a loud noise.

"Whoa!" said Naomi who was bringing a cup of tea and a plate of brownies over for them both.

"Designed to intimidate" said DS Moran still looking at the knife. He folded the blade away and slipped it into a plastic evidence bag. "Which reminds me. We've turned over the Pascoes' place and found all sorts of stuff, passports, phones and cash."

"So will Sonya get anything back?" asked Naomi.

"Yes, we found her passport and wallet" he replied.

"In which case, you can have a brownie!" she said sliding the plate towards him. She was rewarded by a big smile and a flash of those ice-blue eyes.

"Were you a Viking in a previous life?" she asked.

"Er, hello!" said Tom. "I'm beginning to feel like a gooseberry!"

"We'll make sure that Sonya gets her property back, and now I must take a statement from Mr Scobie" he said, trying to look serious, even as he took a bite into one of Naomi's brownies.

"D I Bannister is talking to the Crown Prosecution Service about the Smurfs and the Pascoes. We think there may be evidence of a joint conspiracy there somewhere."

"Which might tie them into the Markham net?" suggested Tom.

"A good chance, it's one of the dots that didn't get joined up by the previous regime" replied DS Moran.

Tom nodded, there were a few loose ends that needed tying up. Something that hadn't happened whilst Markham was able to use his influence locally. After his arrest a new team arrived, including DS Moran.

"Hopefully we can get this wrapped up in time for Christmas" said DS Moran.

"Just going to take a cuppa up to Anna," said Naomi. Anna was resting as part of the regime that Naomi had imposed. They both watched her leave.

"Quite a girl," said Tom.

"You can say that again" replied DS Moran.

34

"This is the life!" Sid was enjoying the business class hospitality on the flight to Sofia. From there he and Tom would take an internal flight to Varna.

"Just don't start any fights!" said Tom, who was also enjoying the in-flight hospitality.

Toddy was going to meet them at the airport and drive them back to his villa. Toddy was going to throw a small party before the main event the following morning. In his own mind Tom recalled when he had been skiing down a very steep slope on the edge of his skis, hearing the sound of the snow and ice crunching beneath him. He had hoped that he wouldn't fall and if he did that nothing would get broken. That's how it felt now.

"This has come together very quickly" he said to Sid just loud enough for him to hear. He had been told by Adam at the briefing meeting that there wouldn't be anybody on the flight who they should worry about.

Sid took a sip of his drink and nodded his understanding. "Quick flash to bang" he said, echoing an old army saying about the suddenness of things.

Tom knew that Toddy's birthday would be the occasion for

the grand signing of his agreement with Don, Darren and the Russians. He had asked Adam for a meeting which had taken place two nights previously in a private dining room in the Covent Garden area. There were some new faces who were also involved in this project. His first request had been to include Sid, who knew most but not all of the story.

"He's my most trusted colleague" he said to Adam, who nodded his approval. You've probably checked him out, thought Tom.

"You'll have Stewart in-country with you" said Adam indicating a neat figure. "I'll fill you in as we go along" he had added. "We can't have an MP getting mixed up in gang-related activity without some top cover."

Stewart McKenzie would be acting as back-up and liaison with the Bulgarian authorities, which to Tom meant that he was Special Forces, probably drawn from the small group that stood by to assist with delicate missions such as this was turning out to be.

And so they had walked through the series of events which they expected to unfold and examined any possible contingencies.

"What do you reckon about the Russkis?" asked Sid. They had dealt with Russians when they were both involved in the NATO task force.

"They won't want any trouble," said Tom. "I'm dubious about this Darren character, he seems to be in with a bunch of locals who would love to take over their side of the operation. That's why I want to make sure that I get to talk privately with Toddy this evening."

"If Toddy signs that deal, does he fall into the hands of the SFO?" asked Sid.

"I hope I was able to persuade the Serious Fraud Office person that Toddy could be a useful ally, rather than making him a suspect. That would make matters worse and push Toddy away from us."

He left the thought hanging in the air as the cabin crew began to clear away prior to landing. The next flight would be less luxurious, but Toddy's hospitality would make them both feel welcome.

He closed his eyes and dosed as the plane descended.

* * *

"Big day tomorrow!" said Darren as he handed Ruslan a tumbler of whisky. Ruslan nodded and took the glass. They were meeting at a hotel bar in Varna that evening.

"*Nazdrovie*" Darren said as they drank.

Darren was a little bit afraid of the big Russian, but they were keen that the deal with Toddy went through. His role was to keep both Don and Toddy sweet, so that they could be locked into the deal.

Both he and Don were in the same boat; they both needed this deal to succeed but they were only brokers. The big money lay with the Russians and the Bulgarians.

"What do you think about Nikolay Todorov?" Ruslan asked. Never one for small talk, thought Darren.

"Useful" replied Darren, struggling to find something to say.

"Why useful? How useful?" Two questions in one. Darren took a sip of his whisky to give him time to think.

"His ambition is to get elected to Parliament, which could be useful" Darren began. He was pleased to see Ruslan nod his agreement.

"We must see that he gets elected" said Ruslan as if he was checking off a to-do list.

"He has a local presence which will be useful as we build up the operation, sorry, project" added Darren. He knew that the

Russians were going to use the casino as a front for their wider operations in the region.

Again Darren was pleased to see Ruslan nod his agreement.

"And this man Scobie, what do you think?" Darren recalled something Don had said.

"Trouble-maker" he replied. He hoped that was an adequate response.

"How trouble?"

Darren had to be careful how he replied. He didn't want Ruslan and his associates to feel that he was not fully in control of the situation.

"You know that Scobie was at the same school as Todorov in England?" he began. Ruslan nodded. "Scobie wants to pull Todorov out of the deal so that he won't be prosecuted by the British authorities."

Ruslan looked puzzled. Darren explained that as a UK citizen Toddy could be implicated in criminal proceedings. That would expose them all to a risk, now that Bulgaria was in the EU. They could be extradited to face justice in the UK.

"Not me" said Ruslan with a smirk. "I am not covered by EU law."

They both took a sip of their drink. Each was waiting for the other to speak first. Ruslan made a face as if he had tasted something that didn't agree with him.

"So maybe Mr Scobie should have an accident," said Ruslan.

35

"Do you think Tom can pull this off?" Georgina said as she poured a cup of coffee for Matt. It was his first visit to her 'skunk works' in Didcot. They had agreed with Tom that they would be the Red team, checking over the plans and advising where they could see gaps in the way things were unfolding.

In reality they both felt this effort was an exercise in displacement activity as there was little they could do to be of practical use to Tom. They walked over to a plain office table where Gloria was guarding a plate of biscuits.

"All of a sudden the gannets appeared!" she said, as her colleagues wandered past helping themselves. They arranged themselves around the table which was covered with papers, laptops and a diminishing supply of biscuits.

"To answer your question, Georgina...." Matt began.

"Call me Georgie" she interrupted, "everybody does."

"Well, yes he can" replied Matt. "Tom has a very high EQ, you know? High Emotional Intelligence. He is good with people and can read the room, as they say."

He then retold the story of the time that Tom led his recce

platoon into the camp of a notorious warlord by mistake when he was on his first tour of duty in the Balkans.

"He told them that he was the advance guard of a bigger group coming their way. They could surrender to him, or die fighting against superior odds."

"I can quite imagine!" said Georgie with a smile.

"They withdrew from their camp, which Tom and his team then dismantled, capturing some very useful papers and radios along the way."

"I never heard that!" said Gloria chuckling.

"He can also look after himself if he has to, he made sure that his blokes got aikido training before they went on operations as they could find themselves in tight corners and weapons were not the answer."

"Anyway...." said Georgie. "Let's see where we've got to."

Matt noted Georgie's constant fidgeting and judged her to be an unquiet soul. Something was driving her, he would have to delve a little deeper but this was not the time.

"It seems that tomorrow is the big day" began Matt. "We know most of the players, we now have to judge how we think they will respond to what unfolds."

"I'm worried that Toddy will fold," said Georgie. "Everything I've heard tells me that he's after money and fame."

"Not quite" said Matt gently, not wishing to bruise her ego. "Tom believes that Toddy wants to restore his family name in the eyes of his community. They were hounded out by the communist regime and now he has the chance for, what, reparation."

Matt explained that Tom was hoping to persuade Toddy to honour his family by not signing a deal that would allow the opening of a casino that could be used for criminality. He could agree to the resort which would bring jobs and tourists to the area. It would demean his family name if a casino was opened which brought in drugs and was a base for trafficking girls.

"We still have the Proton account up our sleeve" added Georgie. "I hope your colleague can do his stuff on the person you mentioned."

"I've had a long chat with my contact," said Matt. "He understands the sensitivities involved. We're not in the business of ruining people's lives or careers, so we have agreed on a means by which we can achieve the effect we want. But you'll have to trust me."

"That sounds like really is serious stuff" said Gloria, breaking the tension.

"Deadly serious," said Matt.

* * *

"Listen, Mr Darren" began Boyko, a swarthy looking man with a gaucho style moustache. "We trust you to find us a good deal. We know Nikolay and his family, they good people, but these *Russkis*, nothing but trouble."

They were sitting in the lounge of a hotel in Varna. Darren had worked hard to bring some Bulgarians into the deal he was putting together with Nikolay Todorov. Ruslan had got wind of the deal and offered to join forces. It looked like a win-win to Darren. Don brought the prospect of more investment, no questions asked. Perfect.

But now the Bulgarians felt they were being marginalised by the Russians and they were angry with Darren. The whole deal could fall apart if the Bulgarians withdrew, as Nikolay would probably follow their example.

Darren nodded as he took a sip of his beer. It gave him time to think. He had a sneaking suspicion that Boyko was putting on a show for the benefit of his two colleagues who were also drinking their beer. He didn't like the way they were looking at him.

"There is a way that everybody wins in this deal," said Darren. He was trying to keep his eyes on Boyko, but the others leaned in to hear what he had to say and that threw him off. He felt that he was losing control of the situation.

"We will deal directly with Nikolay Todorov, Mr Darren, we understand each other." Boyko's tone sounded final. "You English are shopkeepers but you are not deal-makers, not in the way we do *bizness* here."

"We are so close, Boyko," said Darren. He believed that Boyko was bigging himself up. He needed to remind him and his colleagues that they were on the verge of signing a big contract.

"Once we have signed the contract...."

Boyko put his hand up to stop Darren speaking. "No contract, nothing on paper. We have an agreement between partners here" he said. "No signing of any paper" he repeated in case Darren didn't get the message.

Darren blinked. He was going to be left with nothing. The Russians would not be pleased and he would get no fee for brokering the deal.

"You tell your *Russki* friends that we will be all Bulgarians together. Your *Angliski* friend too, we have the way to do this" Boyko said.

Boyko made a gesture to show that the meeting was over. His two colleagues stood up and not in a friendly way. Darren drained his drink and turned to walk out. He needed to preserve his dignity amidst a room full of people who seemed to sense what had just happened. He turned back and saw that the three men had sat down and were in the process of ordering more drinks.

As he walked out of the hotel into the warm evening

sunshine he realised that he would have to have a difficult conversation with his Russian colleagues.

Or he could just disappear.

* * *

"What does this *mean*, Darren?" Don's expression was a mixture of outrage and fear. As he and Darren sat in his hotel room after Darren's meeting with the Bulgarians, Don felt the ground opening beneath him. Things were not going the way he had expected.

"It means that we need to rethink matters" said Darren as he helped himself to a whisky from Don's mini bar.

Don's mind had gone into survival mode. He had managed to evade the police when they came to arrest Lord Markham, and he had managed to make himself useful to Markham once he was locked up. He had the money in a safe place so he could continue to operate on Markham's behalf. He might just need to do another rapid exit.

"I think Boyko wants a bigger slice of the pie" said Darren as he sipped his drink.

Don could see that Darren was trying to work out how he at least would come out smiling. He needed to ensure that he wouldn't find himself out in the cold.

"First thing, we say nothing to the Russians" continued Darren. He drained his glass and went back for another whisky.

"Interesting" said Don. He wondered if Darren had a cunning plan or whether he needed time to think.

"Survival" responded Darren. "I think we can broker a deal directly between Nikolay and the Russians."

"Cut the Bulgarians out, you mean?" Don needed to understand this plan. "Do we think we have a good enough relationship with Nikolay to convince him to renege on his side of the deal?" he asked. "I'm worried that he has fallen under the spell of Scobie."

"So, if we get rid of Scobie, we get rid of the problem?" asked Darren.

Don nodded.

"We can still make sure that we get a good cut," said Don. He was trying to think his way through the problem. "We can act as honest brokers and get the Bulgarians to agree to front for the Russians. Everybody's a winner!"

Darren took another swig of his drink as he tried to piece together Don's line of thought. "This just might work" he said. He didn't believe in Don's proposal, but he was prepared to let him make the running. One thing they did agree on was the need to ensure that Tom Scobie was not part of the picture.

36

"This is going to be some party" said Sid. He and Tom had been given a room each in Toddy's villa. Their host had been his usual effusive self when he greeted them on their arrival. Tom and Sid had been driven from the airport by one of Toddy's drivers, so they kept their conversations to humdrum matters.

"Fill your boots, guys!" Toddy had said once they arrived. "I've got to get tomorrow sorted out. See you later!"

"I need to have a word with Toddy before it gets too late, and before anybody can get at him," said Tom.

Sid had already done a sweep of the room with a clever gadget that detected bugs. It looked like a small transistor radio so didn't attract the curiosity of the airline security staff, who Sid reckoned could be a bit light-fingered.

"We need to know what the timings are tomorrow, so I can brief Stewart" Sid said.

"You two!" said Tom. It turned out that they had both been on the same sniper course back in the day. Stewart had disappeared into the Special Forces world whilst Sid had returned to the recce platoon.

"Nice to know he's got our backs," said Sid. Stewart had said at the briefing meeting that he and colleagues would be providing what he referred to as overwatch. They would only get involved if things became dangerous. Tom was a British MP after all. The diplomatic niceties would be handled by the Embassy in the capital, Sofia.

"I need to have a chat with Georgie and Matt to understand how they think we should handle the question of the Proton account," said Tom.

"If there is no money in the bank Don has no bargaining power" he continued. "His side of the deal falls apart and I think the others may get spooked and fold."

"Where does that leave Toddy?" asked Sid. "He's built his whole world around making this deal work."

"It leaves him sitting on some prime real estate which anybody would be happy to develop," said Tom. "This deal has shut anyone else out for the time being, but I'm pretty certain he'd be knocked down by the rush of other developers who'd sign a deal."

"He'd lose face," said Sid. "You know how things work in this part of the world."

Tom nodded as he took a drink of his beer. "I'll have to persuade him that there is a new chapter he can write for himself, not one being written by a bunch of crooks."

"And nasty ones at that" added Sid. "How would this help to wrap up that toe rag Markham?"

"The proton account represents most of his assets, as far as we can tell," said Tom. "Without that he has no power. If Don can be persuaded to co-operate, so much the better."

"What are the chances?" Sid looked sceptical.

Tom made a face. His knowledge of human nature put Don into the category of chancer. If he saw a way out of this dilemma, he'd take it. He would need to co-operate with the authorities and possibly go into a witness protection programme. "Fifty – fifty" he said.

At that moment there was a tap on the door. Tom walked over to open it. There was a petite brunette outside. "Meester Tom" she began. "Nikolay says to come and join him pleez!" She looked past Tom towards Sid. "Yourself only" she said.

Tom finished the remains of his drink and put the glass on the table. He waved at Sid who appeared to be interested in the figure in the little black dress. "See you later" he said.

"I hope so!" Sid replied giving the girl a wolfish smile.

She led Tom to the poolside den which he remembered from a previous visit. Nikolay had heard him approach and came out to meet him with his characteristic smile.

"Welcome back to my den!" he said. "I have some fizz open so we can drink while we talk!"

He led Tom inside and pulled a bottle of champagne out of its bucket and poured them both a glass. Tom caught sight of the label and noted it was real champagne, not the local fizz.

"So, Tom!" said Toddy as they clinked glasses, "let us speak of cabbages and kings!"

"Good idea, Toddy," said Tom. "There is much for us to talk about."

"Just like that?" said Georgina. "It seems too easy!"

She and Matt were still in the skunk works with Gloria. The rest of the team had mostly gone home earlier. There were still one or two of Georgina's elves, as she called them, in the office working with her on the Markham case.

"Not quite so simple" said Matt. "I've had to pull a few strings to orchestrate this so that our contact at the bank will appear blameless."

Georgina walked over to the coffee pot and discovered it was empty. She put her mug down, waving Gloria who had stood up back to her seat. She didn't really need any more caffeine.

"Once again, please" she said.

"There will be a power failure in the building where the bank is situated" Matt began. "All of the systems will switch off and go into a safe standby mode." Georgina and Gloria nodded. So far so good. "Only when the system is restored will it be discovered that a bug has got into the bank's system."

"And the Proton account is affected by this?" asked Gloria, warming to the idea.

"All the accounts will be, but once the system is debugged, the Proton account will disappear" he said.

"No fingerprints?" asked Georgina.

"Where will the money be?" asked Gloria.

"In a bank in Gibraltar which is monitored by HMG" he said, referring to the UK government.

"Well, aren't you the sneaky one!" said Georgina.

Matt put his forefinger to his lips.

"Don't ask" he said.

37

Tom wasn't sure if Toddy had already had a bit too much fizz, as he prattled away about the plans he was about to realize. "When you have nothing, Tom, all you have is your honour" he said, taking a pull from his glass and refilling it from the bottle in the cooler.

They had got through the pleasantries and Tom was having trouble finding a way into a conversation. Did Toddy know that he was here to dissuade him from going through with the deal? Was his stream of consciousness really a way for him to justify his actions to Tom, and to himself?

"Honour?" He picked up on that word whilst Toddy was drinking.

"Respect" Toddy said.

"Respect is what you earn, Toddy," said Tom. He kept his voice at a low level, almost a whisper making Toddy strain to hear.

"Easy for you, Tom," said Toddy. "You haven't had to rebuild your family name from nothing. My parents and grandparents were enemies of the people. What did Stalin call them? Class traitors."

Tom could see that the drink was pushing Toddy towards a dark place. He was dredging up old resentments. "There's a new regime now" he said, trying to bring Toddy back to the present instead of wallowing in the past.

"Lots of people from the old regime have discovered 'democracy' because it's capitalism and that means money. And money buys you respect in this country!"

That much was true thought Tom. He needed to put Toddy on the spot about the deal he was hoping to sign. He had a good idea that the deal would elevate him in his own eyes to the level of the new oligarchs who were calling the shots these days.

Toddy was not going to be receptive to appeals to his better nature. Not in this mood, so Tom decided on another approach. "We've known each other a long time, Toddy, so whatever you decide now I'll walk beside you." Tom hoped that this sentiment would keep the door open to enable him to offer advice when necessary and warnings when needed. He was glad when Toddy put his glass down and advanced towards him and enfolded him in a bear hug.

"The only one I can trust!" he said as he slapped Tom on the back.

Further back slapping was interrupted by the petite brunette knocking on the door of Toddy's den. Toddy disengaged himself and opened the door. Tom could hear her speaking in a hurried tone of voice as if something had happened. Tom could see that Toddy was not pleased. He looked at Tom.

"The Russians want a meeting" he said in a tense voice. "They are thinking of pulling out. They think that Don is going to do a deal with Boyko, who you haven't met, one of my countrymen who has a lot at stake in this deal."

Tom was thinking on his feet as he didn't have the full picture about who was involved in the deal. "Can you go ahead without the Russians?" he asked.

"They bring money and they will bring in the clientele for the resort and the casino" Toddy replied.

"Why would this chap Boyko not want them involved?"

Toddy shrugged his shoulders and made a face.

"Perhaps you should meet Boyko before you meet the Russians," said Tom.

Toddy nodded and spoke to the young lady in a commanding manner. She seemed to understand her instructions and left closing the door behind her.

Tom was puzzled by this development. He sensed that Don had thrown his lot in with the shady character Darren, who had brought the Russians into the deal. He knew that Toddy was right, the Russians would be the larger partner in this deal. Why would Boyko and his associates want to sink the deal at this late stage?

He needed to know more about Boyko, he had been concentrating on Don and the Markham connection and not paying attention to the other players in the deal. "What is Boyko's story"? he asked Toddy.

"From the Nomenklatura families" Toddy began. He was referring to the entrenched communist bureaucracy who ran the country under the old regime. "Did very well under the old regime and are now doing very well in the capitalist era" he explained.

"Has he got a problem with the Russians being involved in this deal?" asked Tom. As well as helping him to get a handle on what was happening, Tom was hoping that Toddy would be able to think his way through this latest development; but he could see that the drink was slowing down his thinking. "Maybe put them off until tomorrow, give yourself time to think a bit."

"I told the girl...." Toddy began. "This is disrespectful way to do business. We will meet in the morning before we sign the papers."

Tom understood that the unfortunate colleague would be telling the Russians and Boyko that there would be no meeting tonight. "We all need to sleep on it," said Tom. He needed to report back on what was unfolding, to see how they could keep Toddy from signing anything that would incriminate him under UK law, and if there was scope for him to persuade Don to come over to the side of the righteous.

* * *

"Okay" said Darren. "I've thrown the cat among the pigeons and now nobody trusts anybody!"

"Perfect" said Don. "Now we can orchestrate matters and come out smiling!"

Don had warmed to the way that Darren had seemed able to avoid the cliff edge they had suddenly found themselves confronting. The bigger the size of the deal, the bigger would be the cut that they both got. Plus they would benefit from the money from the casino and the girls, which would keep them comfortable into the future.

Darren had seen Don's greed and played on it. Whatever happened, he was going to see to it that Don got the short end of the stick. But for now he was a useful idiot, so he needed to flatter his ego just a little while longer. "So, tell me about this Markham bloke" said Darren as he reached for another bottle in Don's hotel mini bar.

"Smart guy" began Don. "I know he got put away, but he's got his learned counsel working on an appeal...."

"On what grounds?" asked Darren.

"On the basis of his offshore assets which can keep the average barrister and judge very comfortable"

"Must meet him when he gets out," said Darren. And he meant it.

Darren listened as Don waxed lyrical about his relationship with Markham, but his initial impression was being confirmed. Don needed to show Markham that he could look after his interests until he returned to take over. The wise servant.

We'll see about that, he thought.

38

"I've got to have a better picture of how things are developing," said Tom. "I need a real time picture of what these chaps are thinking."

He was back in his room with Sid. They were both drinking a glass of wine. Sid thought things always looked better after a glass, and right now Tom wasn't going to disagree.

"I've got my laptop – my work laptop" said Sid as he reached into his holdall.

Tom knew that Sid could find a way into the local cell phone network and identify the phones that they were aware of. Tom knew Toddy's and Don's mobile numbers, so he gave them to Sid.

"It'll take me a bit of time, but at least we can then track them. If I get lucky I could read their texts and maybe listen in, but I can't be sure."

Tom nodded his agreement. He chided himself for not thinking of a double-cross at the last moment. "I'm going to check in with Georgina" he said. "She's got Matt with her so maybe they've got some insight that I can't see."

He called her and waited while the phone rang. He just

hoped that she wasn't out of signal range. His mind was racing as he tried to silence the inner voice that told him he'd dropped the ball.

"Tom!" Her voice came through reassuringly clearly. "I've got Matt here with me, I'll put you on speaker."

"I'm on my last slice of pizza!" said Matt in his characteristically no-nonsense tone, but Tom was glad to hear that they were working on things at this late hour. As he explained how things had taken an unexpected turn, he was reassured to see Sid working away on his laptop weaving whatever magic he could. Good, he thought, the team is working together. He began to regain his confidence that they would be able to achieve what they hoped.

"Don't blame yourself, Tom" Matt said. "This is a very dynamic situation and you can't cater for every contingency. We're not so far off-beam that we can't put things right."

Tom was a little puzzled at Matt's optimistic tone.

"We've got some news," said Georgina. "The matter we've been working on has been sorted."

Her veiled speech referred to the Proton account. They were being careful in case they were being listened to. The news that the account had been successfully exfiltrated from the bank where Don had deposited it gave Tom new hope.

"Now I think I can see a way forward" he said. "I need to convince our friend that his pot of gold is no longer at the end of the rainbow."

As he was speaking he saw Sid give him a thumbs-up sign.

"I think I'll give him a call" he said into the phone. "It's now or never for him. If we can reel him in then we might persuade him to be helpful. I just hope he's not so afraid of his situation that he keeps silent."

Tom knew that Markham could find him, even if he was in

prison, and deal with him. He had to be persuaded to go into a witness protection programme.

"Keep us posted," said Georgina. He ended the call.

"Toddy is still in his den," said Sid. "I've got Don at a location in central Varna, I guess that's his hotel. I haven't got voice but I have got their text messages. Toddy's are in Bulgarian, so a bit of a mystery."

"What about Don?" asked Tom.

"Interestingly enough he's just got a text message from a bank." Tom could see Sid's smile.

"Bad news?" he asked.

"Customer services asking him to call. He's on the line now but I can't get into it, not yet anyway."

Tom knew he should strike now while Don was unbalanced by the news about his bank account. He would need to use the car and driver that Toddy had offered him. "Bring your laptop with you, Sid, we're going for a drive."

* * *

Tom asked the driver to take them to the bar at the best hotel in Varna. He reckoned that Don and Darren wouldn't stint themselves on the eve of pulling off a major deal. As they drove Sid kept his laptop open and once they were in Varna he was able to identify the location of Don's phone. It was in the hotel the driver had suggested.

The car drew up to the front door, they got out and walked into the hotel as if they owned the place. The servile doorman reckoned Tom must be a big shot oligarch and opened the door for them as they entered. Tom nodded at him in appreciation. People like him tended to remember unpleasant customers.

"Let's sit in the bar and get a drink" said Tom as he walked through the hotel lobby. Even at this hour there were people hanging around. Probably other drivers or bodyguards, thought Tom. "No sign of him in here" he said as they sat at a table. "Must be in his room."

A waiter approached and they both ordered beers. Tom had chosen a corner table where they could observe what was going on. "I'm going to text him and suggest we meet down here. He won't be worried about meeting in a place where there are plenty of people around," said Tom.

"You go and sit at the bar, I'll stay here and watch your back" said Sid.

Tom had to think what message he could send to Don that would convince him to come and meet him. Don needed to know that Tom was aware of the situation with the Proton account. If could be persuaded that Tom was in a position to restore it to him, he would grab the chance. It would be a measure of how desperate he was if he agreed to meet. If that didn't work, he'd have to go up to his room.

As he was composing his thoughts his phone buzzed. He saw it was a call from Anna. He picked up the phone. "Hi..." he said.

"Tom?" He recognised Naomi's voice. She sounded tense.

"What – is Anna OK?" he asked, trying to keep the anxiety out of his voice.

Sid looked up from his laptop.

"We're on our way to hospital, the medics are worried about the way the baby is sitting in her womb" Naomi said. "Blue lights."

"Is she....?" He began.

"The paramedics are stabilising her as we're driving."

"I'd no idea" he said.

"She didn't want to worry you" Naomi said.

He could hear the reproach in her voice. Where are you when your wife needs you?

"You alright, boss?" He heard Sid's voice and saw his concern.

Tom let his head droop. This was too much. He should drop everything and get the first plane back. He could be home by tomorrow afternoon.

He could hear Naomi speaking to someone who sounded like a medic. The background noise suggested that the siren was on and the ambulance was moving at speed. He heard the sound of the phone being picked up.

"They're going to take her straight into theatre and they hope they can save her and the baby," said Naomi.

39

"You've got a face like a slapped arse!" Darren said. Once again he was in Don's hotel room and enjoying the contents of the minibar. He had seen Don pick up his phone and look at a text message. He had gone into the corridor and made a phone call which didn't sound very positive.

"Trouble at home, Don?" Darren was enjoying this. He had been dubious about Don from the outset, he talked big but was always careful not to commit to anything concrete. He thought of Don as a 'free beer tomorrow' merchant.

Don's silence was concerning. Darren watched as Don went to the minibar and saw what little remained. He poured himself some vodka and downed it. Not good, thought Darren as Don didn't usually drink vodka. "Is there something I should know Don?" asked Darren. His tone of voice signalled both impatience and irritation.

Don knew he had to say something to keep Darren happy. The text told him that his account was unserviceable and asked him to call a certain helpline number. The number was busy. Something had happened at the bank which was supposed to be as safe as houses. He had a bad feeling.

Before he could say anything his phone buzzed, it was a text message. Perhaps from the bank. He looked at the message.

IM IN THE BAR DOWNSTAIRS – I CAN TELL YOU MORE
ABOUT THE PROTON ACCOUNT
ILL WAIT FOR YOU. TOM

Don sensed an opportunity to escape the present unpleasant situation. He waved the phone.

"Got to see a man about a dog" he said. "In the bar."

He got up and pulled on his jacket. Darren nodded. "Don't let him take you walkies" he said with a grin. He reached for his glass and watched as the door closed behind Don.

Darren decided that he would give Don five minutes to get downstairs and then follow him. He had been in the bar and knew where he could stand and see who Don was meeting. If he thought that Don was double crossing him, then he would wait until he came back......

Once Tom understood Anna's predicament his mind went into overdrive. He called Matt who was closest to the scene and who would be able to lend some moral support to Anna, as well as giving him an idea of whether he should get on a plane and fly to her side.

"Okay, Tom, I understand" Matt said slowly. He was thinking through what he could do that would be most helpful. "I'm going to call Lizzie and get her to go to the hospital as she is closer than me. I'm in Didcot and she can get there quickly" he said.

Tom was grateful that Matt was prepared to drop everything. He had no other ideas at the moment.

"Lizzie can get her sister to come and look after the boys, and when I get there we can see what we see."

Tom felt a surge of relief flood through him.

"And Tom" continued Matt, "finish the job. Let us take care of things this end; you do what you went there to do."

"What can I say?" said Tom.

"If it's a boy you can name him after me!" said Matt.

Sid saw Tom smiling as he ended the call. Tom told him of the plans that they had made. It was therapeutic for him to see Sid's approval. "She's a tough kid and he's got smarts" he said.

Tom closed his eyes and he saw Anna's face with her untidy tomboy bob of copper hair and that big smile. He heard himself make a noise that sounded like a moan.

"Chin up, boss!" Sid had drawn closer to him. "Got a job to do, then we can all go home, eh?"

Tom could just about find the energy to nod. He'd never felt so desolate. If he lost Anna and their child what would it all have been for?

Sid put his arm around him. This brought Tom back to his senses. Nobody in the bar seemed to be paying any attention. "Right then," said Tom. He nodded to Sid and picked up his glass and walked over to an empty stool at the bar. As he did so he had a glance at the scene around him. The tables were occupied by men huddled together. Some with an over-made-up woman in a very small black dress.

I just hope this makes a difference he said to himself as he sat down on a barstool. The stools on each side were empty so Don could slide in beside him, if he decided to take the bait.

He knew that he had to concentrate on the matter in hand and trust that Matt would let him know what the situation was with Anna. At least she wouldn't feel he'd abandoned her completely.

The wall behind the bar was mirrored so that he could see

the room behind him, through the display of coloured bottles and glasses. Out of the corner of his eye he spotted movement and turning slightly he saw Don moving towards him. He'd taken the bait. He might be open to an offer that could open up the whole of the Markham network and possibly keep Toddy from falling into the hands of the unsavoury bunch who wanted to get their hands on his property.

Tom felt a surge of adrenaline sweep through him. He recalled a previous meeting with a gang boss, when he had to try and persuade him to come over to the right side and betray his comrades. Well, here we go again, thought Tom. Not that Don was a gang leader so much as a stooge.

"Come and join me" he said, smiling.

He indicated the empty bar stool and Don shuffled on to it silently. His face was expressionless. Tom gestured to the bar tender and Don ordered a vodka.

"Didn't know you were a vodka man" said Tom to open the conversation.

"I'm getting a taste for it" replied Don. "What do you know about the Proton account?"

Straight to the point. That gave Tom a clue as to Don's state of mind. He had scored a bullseye and Don wouldn't be here if he wasn't worried. "I know that it's been cleaned out" Tom replied as the bartender gave Don his drink. "I know where the money has gone."

"What do you want?" said Don, taking a swig of his vodka.

"To talk," said Tom.

"I'm listening."

Tom understood the laconic replies as a sign of someone who was trying to decide which way to jump. He needed to persuade him to jump the right way, but Don would have to decide. So far Don was avoiding eye contact, so Tom turned towards him.

"What do you want, Don?" he said in a low voice, as some others shuffled closely past them.

Sid was nursing his drink and looking around the bar. A group of people leaving the bar briefly obscured his view but once they'd passed he could see that Tom and Don were still at the bar. They seemed to be talking. At first it looked like Tom was doing all the talking but now Don had turned towards Tom. They were both ordering a second drink from the bartender which told Sid that things were moving along. No sign of Don getting up to leave.

Also watching this scene was Darren. He knew where to stand so that he was not reflected in the mirror behind the bar. He stood just outside the entrance but he could watch as Don and Tom were speaking.

"Very cosy" he said to himself.

40

S id watched as Tom and Don stood up. Had Tom sealed the deal? He watched as Tom and Don continued to talk as they walked towards the exit of the bar. Sid kept them in view as they walked. Once they were close to the exit he would move to stay close to Tom.

He watched as Tom put his arm out and patted Don on the back. A signal to Sid that the conversation was over. Don walked away without turning back as Tom turned towards where Sid was sitting. Darren had also spotted the movement so made himself scarce.

As Tom walked back Sid kept an eye on others in the room who might be making moves to follow Don. He saw nothing. As Tom sat down, Sid was finally able to finish his drink. "How was that?" he asked.

"Not in the bag yet" said Tom, looking around to see if anybody was listening.

"I think that he's trying to find a way out that leaves him with the money back in the Proton account and able to do the deal with Toddy and the others."

"Doesn't sound plausible," said Sid.

"He's scared of what might happen if he bails out of the deal. His usefulness to Markham disappears. Not to mention what the others will do if they think he's ratting them out."

"We don't have anything on Markham if he doesn't cough," said Sid. "All of this was for nothing."

"Not quite," said Tom. "If we can keep Toddy out of the hands of the characters that Don is dealing with, we can at least keep him in control of his family reputation. If he can then find other partners he can deal with, it will be reparation for him."

Sid nodded, even though he didn't entirely agree. He knew that Tom had a particular way of looking at things. Maybe Tom could see a bigger picture that he couldn't.

"I'm going to check in with Georgina to see if we have got enough material to finish things with Markham. Now we've got the money into a safe harbour, we might have to be content with a lesser charge."

"And what about Don?" asked Sid. "Does he walk free?"

"No, we can ask the Bulgarians to arrest him now and hope we can get him extradited. What we don't want is him doing a midnight skip to Northern Cyprus where he is safe from extradition back to the UK."

Sid seemed to accept this. As they got up to leave he said that he'd call Stewart once they were back in Toddy's villa. "I'll get him to rev up the Bulgarian *polizei*" he said.

Tom nodded. As they walked out to find a taxi, he looked at his phone for any news from Matt.

Nothing.

* * *

"The Russians want to meet" said Toddy as Tom and Sid walked back into his villa. Tom decided that as he had no news to tell him about Don and his plans, he would concentrate on the situation with the Russians. "What did they say?" he asked.

"They want me to sign a deal with them and not with the Bulgarian people" Toddy replied. "They want you there too".

"What do you think?" asked Tom. He wanted time to work out what this meant. Also it would give him an insight to Toddy's frame of mind.

"It would be like we were being recolonised by Moscow!" he said. "I would be a hostage in my own home if I signed with them. But the Bulgarian side is hesitating."

"What if you decide not to sign any deal?" suggested Tom. This was his preferred tactic. "You're sitting on some pretty good real estate and you'd find others who would buy into the same plan." Sid indicated that he was going to make the calls he had mentioned and Tom waved him away.

"I have to listen to what they say" began Toddy. "I'm honour bound...."

"What time do they want to meet and where?" asked Tom.

"They suggested somewhere private, I said here is good. They say they choose."

Tom smelt a rat. Both he and Sid had got to know the layout of Toddy's villa and worked out where was a safe place if trouble started and where they should avoid. "Remember, Toddy, they want you to sign a deal. You decide to meet them here or no deal."

Tom hoped that Toddy would see the logic of this.

"Remember this is about honour and respect. If you go running after them, you're already a loser."

He saw Toddy's expression harden at the suggestion that he was dancing to the Russians' tune. "Tell the Bulgarians to be here too" Tom added. "Both sides will see that you are calling the shots."

Tom held his breath while Toddy absorbed the idea. Tom hoped he had not overstepped the mark and bruised his ego.

"Of course, Tom, that makes sense. Who do these hooligans think they can push around?" With that Toddy turned on his heel and marched off in the direction of his poolside den. Tom thought about following him but thought better of it. He had said his piece and hovering around Toddy would make it seem like he didn't trust him. He went upstairs and knocked on Sid's door. He told him of the latest developments.

"I haven't got a way into the Russians" said Sid referring to his box of tricks. "I'll have to have a look at Toddy's call list and work it from there."

"He's probably on the line to them now, if you're quick," said Tom.

Sid nodded and started tapping on his laptop. He quickly accessed the programme that monitored the local phone cell traffic and identified Toddy's phone. Having got the number he was calling he could then go into where the phone was.

"Outside of town" he said. "Somewhere north of here. Some hills..."

"Nice dacha country," said Tom. He remembered their drive down from Dobrich and recalled pleasant countryside with some secluded houses. Perfect for a base of operations.

"I don't think we want to go out there" he said. "Too remote. I'll see what Toddy says but I need to tell him it would be dangerous to go there."

41

"It's on!" Darren got a call in the small hours of the morning. He hadn't made up his mind what to do about Don and decided to sleep on it. When he got the call he reckoned that he would be able to see which way Don was going to jump. If he made the wrong call, he would be able to step aside and let matters take their course.

He had mentioned to his Russian colleagues that he was worried about Don's reliability; they had replied that it wouldn't be a deal breaker. What they wanted was Todorov's signature. They felt that he was a weak character and could be led to see the benefit of a business alliance with them. Then they were in control.

He had knocked on Don's door and told him the news. There would be a rendezvous at Todorov's villa. Don had simply smiled and gave a thumbs-up sign.

"Big day tomorrow then," said Don. He didn't know if the choice of the venue was significant. It meant that Toddy would feel he was calling the shots. There was still a chance that things could work out. Given the prospect of a large payday if the deal went through, he felt that all the parties would find a face-saving formula.

He slept well believing that his luck would hold. He had managed to avoid the fate of Lord Markham, who had been arrested, by relying on his wits. The same wits would be deployed now, to ensure that he came out smiling and with Markham's assets increased.

Tom had told him that the Proton account was now under the control of the UK government. But Don had suggested to Tom that without access to the money he would be of no use to him, if he hoped to help Toddy.

Tom had understood this and said that he would ensure that this message was relayed to those 'higher up the chain of command'. That was useful information for Don who often beat Markham at poker. He would have to keep his cards close to his chest tomorrow.

* * *

Tom was fast asleep when he got the call.

"Congratulations, Daddy!" It was Matt's voice.

He felt a surge of relief as Matt told him that he was the father of a healthy daughter. His sense of relief almost stopped him hearing that Anna had undergone an emergency caesarean and was now recovering.

"At least you won't have to name her after me!" continued Matt.

"Matilda?" suggested Tom. They both laughed.

Tom realised that part of his relief was that his feelings of guilt at leaving Anna in her hour of need had not turned into a real drama. He didn't need to fly home, but he resolved to end this matter quickly so that he could meet mini-Scobie in person. It also meant he would have to be on his toes, he had plenty of reasons to want to stay out of trouble. "Tell Anna that this is defi-nitely my last adventure" he said. "I'll be back just as soon as I can."

"Finish the job, Tom" said Matt sternly. "We've all put a lot of effort into this, so reel in Don and keep Toddy out of trouble."

"Will do!" said Tom. They ended the call.

He sat back in his bed and allowed a wave of well-being wash over him. He had a wonderful wife and now he had a precious daughter to look after. His mind was full of a thousand thoughts about their future lives together. Things they would do, places they would go.

Above all he would have to be more attentive to family life. Anna had followed him on his quest to frustrate Markham's plans to hijack the election and put his own preferred candidate in place. She had gone through a lot during the campaign and then he had gone straight off to a life in Westminster. He would need to think about what he could do so that he could spend more time with his family.

He suddenly felt exhausted. He looked at the time and made sure that his alarm was set for an early wake- up later. He needed to have a serious talk with Toddy before the arrival of all the parties to the signing of the contract.

* * *

"Any idea about names?" said Sid as they helped themselves to the breakfast buffet Toddy had arranged on the terrace.

"I'm still getting used to the idea," said Tom.

"Good to see you in a better mood!" replied Sid.

Tom nodded. He knew that he had almost blown several months of effort. As he helped himself to the breakfast pastries he felt ashamed that he had so nearly let everybody down.

"So let's finish the job, eh?" said Sid reading his thoughts.

"Does Toddy know? That'll be an excuse for another bottle of fizz!"

Tom's head was still reeling but he put that down to the cold shower he had endured to wake himself up.

One of the household staff came in to check that all was well with their breakfast. When he asked, Tom was told that Toddy was still asleep.

"Probably just as well" said Tom as he took a sip of his much-needed coffee. Once they were alone again, he shared his concerns about Toddy with Sid. "I knew he was a bit of a boozer, but lately he seems to be permanently on the bottle. I'm worried that it's clouding his judgement."

"Cracks well under pressure!" said Sid. A remark they had both heard from instructors when on training courses. The target for this remark was usually someone who could do better with a little more effort.

Tom was not yet convinced that he had managed to persuade Toddy to agree with his suggestion. Perhaps the reality of having to take a very important decision was beginning to tell. "He needs to be clear-headed today" continued Tom.

And so do, I he thought.

42

"Who is betraying whom?" said Sid as he took in the scene before him.

Tom was told by Tanya who seemed to be Toddy's companion and general helper, that he would meet them all on the terrace. The air was still cool and the morning was fresh, a pleasant change. They heard the sound of a car approaching along the driveway.

"Looks like the Bulgarians are arriving first to stake out their turf," said Tom. "Boyko Dimitrov wants to deal directly with Toddy."

The car carrying Boyko and his associates drove up to the front of the house. Three men got out and the car pulled away to the side of the house. Tom recognised Boyko from the big party that Toddy held in the summer. "Come and join us!" he said, waving towards the buffet spread.

"Ah! Mr Tom – old school friend, I remember you!" replied Boyko jovially.

They shook hands and Boyko waved his two colleagues towards the buffet. As there was no sign of anybody else the two stooges started examining the buffet.

"Always good to meet friends" continued Boyko. They made small talk as they walked along the buffet. Tom allowed Boyko to do all the talking as he tried to understand what sort of person he was. He seemed like many of the *bizzniss* men he had met during his time in the region. He wore a short-sleeved shirt while his two colleagues had jackets on. Tom assumed that they were armed.

"Who is this?" said Boyko as another smaller car drew up. It turned out to be Darren driving an incongruously small car. He and Don got out of the vehicle. One of Toddy's staff appeared and waved them towards the side of the house. Darren got back into the car, leaving Don to walk into the terrace alone.

"Well, well, Mr Scobie, fancy seeing you here," said Don. Tom could see that he was looking around him warily, as the others were also sizing him up. "I thought I might stop by for a dip in the pool" Don added.

The staff member waved Don towards the buffet. As he walked over, Boyko moved closer to Tom. "Who are these clowns?" he asked.

"They're harmless" he muttered. Boyko's smile was more a smirk of derision.

Presently Darren walked onto the terrace. With his wrap-around shades he looked every inch the dodgy second-hand car dealer, which Tom had discovered was what brought him to this region. He used to sell on stolen cars. "Jack the lad," said Tom. He had to explain the reference to Boyko.

Looking up he saw Sid was looking in the direction of the driveway, as the sound of an approaching car got louder. Tom walked back in his direction and turned to see two black Mercedes saloons drive in.

"Looks like the Russkies have arrived in force," said Sid.

Tom had not met Ruslan before now but he recognised him from a picture he'd seen at their briefing meeting back in

London. Like Boyko, Ruslan was escorted by two well-built and jacketed sidekicks. Both Tom and Sid noticed that no one got out of the other car even though there were people still inside it.

"Doesn't look good," said Sid. "Why is that car sitting there?"

"Looks like he's come with back-up" said Tom in a low voice. "Now might be a good time to warn Stewart that we might need his services."

One reason Tom was glad that the meeting was taking place at Toddy's villa was that Stewart had been able to do a recce of the area and had recommended some useful escape routes and some hiding places in case "things kick off".

Sid slid away around a corner to send a message to Stewart. Tom was watching as the various groups picked at the breakfast buffet and withdrew to their own safe spaces. He thought they looked like animals around an African watering-hole.

Was Toddy going to be the bait, or was he the hunter?

* * *

"Finally....." said Tom as they saw Toddy making a grand entrance onto the terrace. Behind him came Tanya wearing what she thought was a dress for business. A little black dress which didn't suit the occasion or the increasingly warm weather. She was also carrying a black leather folder, which Tom supposed must be the contract they were all here to sign.

Tom noticed that Don was moving towards him, looking like he wanted to say something.

"Lovely Tanya has been keeping me fully informed about Toddy's plans" he said in a matter-of-fact voice. That caught Tom's attention. Was he bluffing? "I know what he wants to do. You seem to be the person he trusts. If you let me have the Proton account back, I can cut you in on the deal and we will both be very rich" Don continued.

Tom met his gaze with a poker face. Don couldn't read what this meant so he continued in the same vein. "We'll get a signing percentage of the contract price, a very handy sum, and the continuing revenue from the resort into the future. Should make you and the family very comfortable."

Tom nodded and smiled. Don had just revealed to him how much he needed the Proton account back in his hands. Without it none of these treasures could be his.

"Don't forget, Don, the account is in a very safe place." Tom resumed his examination of the various people picking their way through the breakfast buffet. As he was speaking they were joined by Darren who had managed to find a glass of beer. A bit early, thought Tom.

"Oi, oi!" he said raising his glass. "Think we met here one fine evening" he said to Tom, reminding him that they had all met at the same party.

"Just so," said Tom. He couldn't see past Darren's mirror sunglasses but he maintained his poker face.

"I know that you've extracted the Proton account, Mr Scobie, but I also know who did it for you. The Swiss police will not look kindly on a case of economic sabotage. It damages their reputation. All they'd have left is chocolate and cuckoo clocks" he continued with a sneer.

Tom was pretty certain that both Darren and Don were bluffing, as they needed to get their hands back on the Proton account. Without it Don would have nothing and Darren would have to choose who he sided with. Not fatal, but a blow to his prestige in this very status-conscious region. Even so he couldn't take the chance. He needed to double-check with Matt and Georgina that all was well.

"Well, let me see what I can do" he said as he turned away from them and walked over to where Sid had just finished his call to Stewart. "Those two clowns look very pleased with themselves" Sid said with a puzzled expression. "Something I should know?"

"I need to check with Matt and Georgina that their contact is safe" Tom replied in a matter-of-fact voice.

"Oh?" Sid's alarmed tone reminded Tom of what was at stake. If someone had managed to interfere with Matt's source or somehow compromised it, things would look very different. Only once he had spoken to Matt would he be one hundred percent sure that all was well.

Amidst the rising hubbub Tom made a call to Matt. He and Sid watched as the gathered group crowded around Toddy to make small talk. They all wanted him to sign the contract for their own reasons.

Tom waited as Matt's phone rang. After what seemed like an eternity Matt picked up. "Tom?" he began.

Tom recounted the conversation he had just had and asked Matt if he was in a position to double-check that his source was safe.

"I'll need to check" said Matt, who understood the importance of what Tom had just told him.

"And Matt" added Tom "please make sure that you're all safe. These folks know what is at stake, so please get in touch with D I Bannister and ask her if she can initiate Op Ridgeway – she'll understand." They ended the call.

"Op Ridgeway is something that Izzy Bannister and I talked about after the election. It is a visible police presence close to my family to protect them from any blowback from Markham's cronies. I wouldn't put anything past this lot."

43

Matt looked puzzled. The number that he used to call his contact regarding the Proton account was unobtainable. A mechanical voice told him that the number was not recognised.

"Trouble?" asked Lizzie who was back from the hospital where they had been looking after Anna and the new baby girl. Naomi and Mike had relieved her.

"Not sure," said Matt. "I think my contact might have chosen to go dark after the recent episode with the account he was managing."

Lizzie was used to Matt taking calls from strangers in the middle of the night as part of his work on reconciliation, acting as a go-between.

He told her of his call from Tom earlier in the morning. He had called Izzy Bannister and she agreed to implement Op Ridgeway. She called back almost immediately to say that DS Moran and a response car were on their way to the hospital where Anna and baby were.

"I need to call Georgina and bring her up to speed" he added. "She's completely wrung out by all of this. She's still grieving for her colleague Jack and blames herself every time there's a setback."

"Is this a setback?" asked Lizzie who could not keep her concern out of her voice.

"Seems like Tom is in the middle of a three-way stand-off" said Matt trying to sound nonchalant. He was trying to reassure Lizzie whilst trying to imagine how he could get in touch with his contact.

In previous cases where contact had been broken, he had managed to resume contact by casting his net wider and finding another means to get in touch. He would have to do something similar now.

"You know how resourceful Tom is" he said, in what he hoped was a reassuring manner. "I just need to be sure about the person who manages the proton account. They may not be so savvy as Tom is" he added.

His phone buzzed and he snatched it off the table-top where he had put it down. His nerves were jangling and he saw Lizzie's worried expression.

It was Mike, Tom's brother, not his contact. "Er, nothing to worry about" Mike began. Matt was worried. "One of the nurses just told me that she saw some strange folks wandering the corridors that she didn't recognise." Matt's blood ran cold. "She said they had lanyards on with 'contractor' but they were definitely snooping around, as if they were looking for something."

"Keep close to Anna and look out for the coppers who are on their way to you now" said Matt, trying to stay calm. Lizzie drew closer to him, so that she could hear what was being said.

"Naomi is with Anna and she can look after herself!" said Mike.

They both chuckled at that. It was certainly true as they had all heard about the incident with the dog as Sonya had made her escape.

"Let me know when the coppers arrive" said Matt and they ended the call.

Now he needed to retrace the network of contacts he had used to reach the person who managed the Proton account. He had seen the media coverage that mentioned an 'IT problem' at the bank concerned but there had been no mention of missing money or of any suspicion falling onto employees. Well, there wouldn't be, thought Matt, a Swiss bank wouldn't wash its laundry in public.

* * *

Tom looked at his watch. He was too tense to eat any more food, so he had been wandering around playing with a cup and saucer. Occasionally he allowed himself another trip to the coffee pot. Sid intercepted him as he was walking around and drew alongside him.

"I reckon at least one of the Bulgarians has got a shooter up his sleeve. Same again for the Russkis. I can't guess what's in the car, maybe two……"

"Keep an eye on lovely Tanya" muttered Tom as he took a sip of his coffee. "She's got the paper they all want Toddy to sign. He's doing a good job glad-handing everybody, playing quite a good game from what I can see."

Sid nodded and headed off towards where Tanya was standing by herself at an occasional table nibbling at a pastry. Tom kept an eye on her body language as Sid approached. She looked up and smiled at him, probably grateful for the distraction of having someone to talk to.

His phone buzzed, it was Matt, and he saw a text message.

ALL WELL – HAVE RESTORED CONTACT AND SPOKEN – NO TROUBLE WITH PROTON

He smiled as he read the text. He looked up and saw that both Darren and Don had been watching. He raised his coffee cup and nodded in salute to them and was rewarded by a scowl in return.

He caught Sid's gesture as Tanya was summoned to join Toddy. Tom walked over to where Sid was, taking the long way around the terrace and the pool so that he could have a good look at everybody. He could feel the adrenaline beginning to work, or was it the coffee?

"We're on!" said Sid.

44

It's a funny thing, thought Anna, as she sat in her bed in her room in the hospital. The familiar sounds she had got used to when she worked in A & E in Glasgow sounded like an orchestra warming up before a concert. Peeps and trills from various medical monitoring devices, the warble of a telephone.

Here she was a new mother recovering from her delivery, nurses and doctors asking her 'How are you feeling?' How are you supposed to feel when you've just brought a new life into this world?

The wee bundle – mini-Scobie - was lying at the foot of her bed in her cot sleeping. She couldn't wait for Tom to meet her. They could think about a name in due course

Mike and Naomi had been given permission to be close at hand, but the medical staff insisted that she should be allowed to rest and heal after her delivery. She closed her eyes and dozed off.

"I'm going in search of some coffee" Mike said to Naomi, who nodded and went back to reading her book.

"Good morning." Naomi looked up as the door opened, and she saw D S Moran standing in the doorway.

"I deny everything!" she said with a smile. She noticed his preoccupied manner.

"Everything alright?" she asked, noting his concern.

Anna stirred in her bed. She saw D S Moran and waved at him wearily and closed her eyes again. He moved closer to Naomi.

"We're just a bit worried that some of the bad guys might be prowling around here. We think they might try to snatch the lady, plus babe, to coerce Tom to do things their way. Sit tight here, please. Where is the brother…?"

"You mean Mike? He went to get some coffee from the machine down the hall." She tried not to let her anxiety show in her voice and disturb Anna.

"They'll have to get past me!" she said, recovering herself.

"That's my girl!" he said. "I've got some uniform colleagues on their way and they know which room you're in. I'm just going to have a prowl around here to see if I can spot any faces I know, or people whose faces don't fit."

He shut the door behind him as he left. He checked the room number and noted that there was no name of the patient outside the door. Reassured that all the rooms looked alike, he took a moment to look up and down the corridor. He moved away from the door to give himself a better view.

There was a steady traffic of medical staff, cleaners, volunteers and contractors walking through the corridor. Nobody seemed to pay any attention to him as they were preoccupied with their immediate concerns. A patient was wheeled past him, and he had to make room for the bed to pass him. No sign of the brother, who he thought he would recognise.

He spotted a man and a woman wheeling a chair purposefully along the corridor. Unlike others he had been watching, who were ambling along, these two looked intent upon a mission. He remained still, not wishing to draw attention to himself. Unlike the other people passing by, the couple were on the lookout. They paid him no attention, perhaps they thought he was waiting for something or someone.

When they stopped outside Anna's room he started moving towards them. He reached into his jacket and produced his warrant card. "Police officer...." he began.

The couple turned and ran, abandoning the wheelchair. He reached into his pocket and found his radio.

"All units ref Op Ridgeway, watch out for two people running in the Guthrie wing. Stop on sight. Am remaining with the subject."

His radio squawked as his colleagues responded. He saw Mike approaching from the direction in which the fugitives had fled. He saw Moran and his concerned expression.

"Had to go miles to find a coffee machine. Something up?" he asked.

"Did you get a look at those two who were legging it down the corridor?" Moran asked.

"Er, yes I think so." Mike replied. "Anna OK?"

"Fortunately yes, let's have a look-see." They walked back into Anna's room. Naomi was reading a book and Anna was still snoozing. The baby girl was fidgeting in her cot without a care in the world.

"Stay here, don't let anybody in except me or one of my colleagues" Moran said and turned on his heels, heading along the corridor in the direction the fugitives had taken. His radio squawked into life.

"Boss, we've got two likely looking types, out the back by the staff car park, both resisted arrest."

"On my way" he responded. He stopped a passing porter, showed him his warrant card, and asked where the staff car park was. He was shown a short cut via an outside metal staircase. He ran out to where he found two uniformed police officers and two people lying on the ground with their arms behind their backs.

A quick search revealed a small medical-looking bag with a syringe and a bottle of some sort of medical liquid. "What's all this then?" he asked. "Were you hoping to walk out with Anna Macdonald? What about the others? What were you going to do with them?"

"Boss!" One of the PCs had delved further into the medical bag and found some parcel tape and a cutthroat razor which she was holding out to him.

* * *

Toddy had asked everybody to gather around a small table where Tanya had placed the folder ready for the signing cere-mony. He was now the ringmaster. Tom and Sid stood at the back of the small group. They noted how the various groups had sorted themselves into clusters for mutual safety. They had all been given champagne flutes to toast Toddy's birthday.

Toddy began to speak in Bulgarian; Tom assumed that he was making welcoming remarks. His command of Bulgarian was limited to ordering a beer, so he had to read the body language of the Bulgarians in the audience. "So far so good" he murmured to Sid. "He's blowing smoke at them."

As Toddy continued to speak Tanya moved towards Tom. She too was holding a glass of champagne. Tom could see that she wanted to speak to him, so he moved towards her, the better to hear.

"I don't know what he is going to do now" she whispered to him. "He is in a bad place. He thinks everybody is trying to rob him of his birth right."

Hearing this, Tom thought that the best thing to do would be to force the pace and get to the crux of the matter.

"What is happy birthday in Bulgarian?" he asked. She whispered into his ear.

"*Chestit rozhden den, Nikolay*!" he called out, raising his glass.

Everybody raised their glass and Nikolay followed suit. Tom caught his eye and offered him a friendly wave as if to say – I am here. Nikolay responded with what Tom took to be a friendly enough smile and a wave.

Sid gave Tom a nudge and inclined his head towards one of the Russians who was unbuttoning his jacket.

"Does he know something we don't know?" asked Sid.

45

"Nasty, really nasty" said D S Moran, as Izzy Bannister surveyed the scene in the hospital corridor. Two uniformed WPCs with all their accoutrements, stab vests and squawking radios stood guard outside Anna's room.

"Looks like they were planning on kidnapping Anna and the baby and coercing Tom into releasing Markham's money," said Izzy.

"As for Naomi and Mike...." D S Moran continued. "Doesn't bear thinking about. How did they know she was here?"

"Well, we're going to have to see how talkative they can be once we've got them into a cell." Izzy was all business.

"I've spoken to the journalist, Georgina and Tom's cousin Matt" she continued. "I guess it was no secret that Anna was due, but she came in as an emergency, so someone here must've been on the lookout. You might have a word with the personnel folks about their agency staff."

Moran nodded and walked off to find someone from the admin department to begin his enquiries. Izzy looked at her watch. She was due to be at police headquarters in Kidlington later in the morning, but she couldn't resist a quick peek to see how mother and baby were getting on.

As she opened the door, she saw that Anna was sitting up and feeding her baby girl, while Naomi was busy getting out the baby's clothes. Anna looked up and gave Izzy her biggest smile ever.

"Thought I'd see how you're getting on" she said. "How is the new addition, and how are you?"

"We are both grand, thanks" said Anna, who couldn't stop smiling.

"Er, where's John – your colleague?" asked Naomi. "We never got an explanation for all the fuss."

Izzy wondered how much she should share with them. This was not the time to go into the gruesome detail of what could have happened.

"I think D S Moran just won himself a commendation for quick action, if I have anything to do with it!" she said. "All is well, and we'll get you home safely as soon as the medics can discharge you." With that she gave a little wave and ducked out of the room, not wanting to get drawn into any details.

"OK, ma'am, we've got this" said one of the WPCs as she walked away to her next appointment.

Damn you, Markham, Izzy thought. Just when we thought we had everything tied up neatly….

* * *

"I have a horrible feeling this is going to be just like Mostar," said Tom.

He and Sid had found themselves in the middle of an inter-gang gunfight, whilst they were both working for a NATO task-force in the Balkans in the bad old days. They were able to escape but it was a close shave.

"This is too open for anybody to hide," said Sid. "If they start shooting...." he began.

"It'll be like a circular firing squad, have they any idea....?" said Tom.

"This is not the time for a range safety lecture," said Sid.

"We've got to keep Toddy safe and we need to ensure that Tanya has a hold of that document" said Tom.

Taking their glasses with them, they wove their way through the throng to get close to Toddy. He saw them coming and lifted up a bottle of champagne. Tom decided to play it cool.

"We need to move you to a safe place, Toddy, I think this is about to get ugly" Tom said as Toddy poured them both a glass.

Sid had placed himself in a position to deny anybody a clear shot at Toddy if they tried it. Tom caught Tanya's eye and beckoned her over to join them. "Get hold of the folder and take it into Toddy's den please" he said in a voice that he hoped conveyed a sense of urgency without panicking her. She looked at Toddy, who nodded his agreement, and she turned and went.

Seeing her pick up the folder, Darren put two and two together. He walked up to her "Where are you going with that?" he said as he put his hand on the folder.

"Pleez!" said Tanya, attempting to shake him off.

Others spotted what was going on and began to move towards Toddy, to prevent him from leaving them standing. Tom began to move Toddy towards his den which was just off the terrace. Sid moved towards Tanya to retrieve her and the folder.

"Hands off the lady, matey" he hissed, as he began to move Tanya in the direction of Toddy's den.

Darren maintained his grip on Tanya. "The time for talking is over, let's get this done and we can all go home" he said.

"Change of plan," said Sid.

"What's going on?" demanded Don who had come over to

find out what was unfolding. He had been watching the scene unfold.

"*Predatel!*" shouted one of the Russians angrily at Toddy – Traitor.

Both Don and Darren began to jostle Tanya, trying to move her away from Sid and to grab the folder. Toddy saw what was happening and yelled something at them in Bulgarian that sounded to Tom like a challenge to their manhood.

He broke loose from Tom's guiding hand and waded into the melée and started throwing punches. The sound of breaking glass and tables being overturned meant that there would be no signing today. Tom spotted Ruslan making a signal to the car that was still parked in the driveway. Two more stooges got out of the car and began moving swiftly towards the crowd. Tom guessed they were going to strong-arm Toddy into the back of their car, drive off with him and hold him hostage until he signed the papers.

"Sid!" he yelled. "Got to get her in the den" he said, pointing towards the approaching stooges. At which point Sid began swinging punches at the group around him which broke Darren's grip and stunned Don, who stood still as if he couldn't believe what was happening. He pushed Tanya who needed no urging towards Toddy's den.

Tom pushed his way towards Toddy and took a couple of punches in the process. His boxing training helped him to roll with the punches, so he didn't lose his balance. "In the den Toddy – *now*!" somehow his words had a galvanising effect on Toddy, who broke off punching people and followed Tom.

The Russians spotted that their opportunity to grab Toddy was disappearing. "*Stoi!*" yelled Ruslan – Stop! To emphasize his point, he fired a single shot into the air. This momentarily stunned the crowd, but only for a short while. Both Tom and Sid watched as others from both sides drew out their own pistols, determined to preserve their honour.

"Gunfight at the OK Corral" said Sid, as he finally got Tanya into the den.

Tom was still outside the den, trying to shove Toddy into what he hoped would be a safe place. He watched with horror and dismay as Toddy produced his own Makarov pistol. He had come prepared.

Tom heard the familiar slap as a bullet struck the wall beside him, with the simultaneous boom from a pistol that somebody had fired. "Down Toddy!" he yelled, but Toddy had other ideas.

Tom tried to drag him to the ground, but he was intent on defending his honour. Tom saw that one of the Russian stooges was getting close; he too had a drawn pistol. Toddy also spotted him and pointing his pistol in his direction he pulled the trigger.

Tom's heart stopped as he heard the grinding of the pistol jamming. The Russian fired at Toddy from close range. He fell back with the impact of the bullet. His yell of pain and anger told Tom that the wound wasn't fatal. As he fell he dropped his pistol, which Tom grabbed.

Crouching down he cleared the jam and pointed the Makarov towards the Russian and squeezed off what he hoped would be a double tap, one to put him down, one to shut him up.

A very loud noise stunned Tom whose head was spinning.

46

Tom was aware of being grabbed from behind by both shoulders and pulled away from Nikolay who lay on the floor. His head was ringing. He could see figures in black overalls with firearms moving around the terrace. A figure moved in front of him and was speaking at him, but he could hear nothing. He guessed that this was the after-effect of a couple of stun grenades, flash bangs, being used to stun people.

He recognised a Union Jack patch on the right arm of his overall and saw the face of Stewart and another he did not recognise. Stewart gave him a thumbs-up sign, which he just about had the energy to respond to with a nod. He felt as weak as a new-born kitten.

Tom raised his arm and pointed towards Nikolay, Stewart looked in his direction and said something to one of his colleagues who moved over to tend to him. He felt a pair of hands behind him pushing him into a more upright position.

He saw Sid and Tanya looking at him; she was speaking to someone wearing a police uniform. Some of the stooges had been sat down on the ground and were being handcuffed. He recognised Darren but could not see any sign of Don.

Tom imagined that his hearing was returning. He spoke and could feel the vibration in his head as he did so. He remembered that the disorientation passed after a time. He tried to stand up and Stewart helped him to his feet. He was led to a nearby chair and sat down.

He saw the coffee pot was still on its stand and pointed towards it, as he asked for a cup of coffee. One of Nikolay's staff was able to provide him with a cup and saucer which Tom thought was out of place, given the scattered tables and chairs around him. Sid moved towards him and started speaking, Tom could hear him – just.

"Might have known you'd go straight for the coffee!" he said. His smile of relief was reassuring.

Tom was glad that he could hear. He took a sip of the coffee which had extra sugar in it as a counter to a possible shock reaction.

"Where's Don?" asked Tom. He feared that he might have managed to get away from the melée.

In response Sid pointed in the direction behind Tom. He turned gingerly to counter the dizziness he was still experiencing. He saw two Bulgarian policemen in the process of retrieving a body from the pool. No doubt about it - Don's features and his clothes were recognisable.

"Did you see what happened?" Tom asked.

"Not sure" Sid began, "but when the shooting started everybody hit the deck apart from Don. Took a couple of shots in the body" he added in a matter-of-fact tone of voice.

Tom was trying to put a picture together of what had just happened. "Was he shot at, or was he caught in the crossfire?" he asked.

"Just unlucky I guess" replied Sid.

They both watched as the dripping body was placed on the ground and a body bag was produced.

"Well, he did say he might take a dip," said Tom.

* * *

"And how are you now, Tom?" Mr Evans was pouring them both a glass of whisky in his Westminster office. The autumn weather was a chilly contrast to the bright sunshine of the Black Sea.

"Getting used to being a dad!" was Tom's first reply.

The reunion with Anna was all the sweeter for the chance to meet his new daughter. Anna was back at home and Naomi had taken on the role of helper whilst Anna was still recovering.

"I did a debrief in Sofia at the Embassy and I must have given the same statement about four times to different people" Tom added.

Evans nodded and tapped a paper on his desk, a copy of his statement. "So many agencies involved" he explained. "HMG, Customs, Bulgarian, Swiss, and on... The character Darren is being extradited back to the UK by the Bulgarians, they don't want his kind in their country."

"And the Russian lot?" asked Tom.

"Being repatriated" replied Evans. Tom wasn't quite sure what that meant. "The Special Forces team were watching what was going on" Evans continued. "There was a lot of radio traffic about whether they should intervene, but once the shooting began they had to get you out."

"Probably saved my life" said Tom, reflecting on a very narrow squeak. "Now I have a family to consider. When I was younger, I was ready to take on all-comers; now I'm not so sure." He took a sip of his whisky.

"I'm glad to hear that your friend Nikolay is on the mend" added Mr Evans. "He somehow managed to come out of this smelling of roses. Something of a local hero."

"It's reparation for him, he's restored his family honour without the need to do dodgy deals" explained Tom.

"You have been told about the attempt to kidnap your wife and child?" Evans asked.

Tom nodded. It was too gruesome to contemplate. He would have been forced to return the Proton account to Don and there was no guarantee that Anna would have been safe afterwards. There seemed to be no end to Markham's capacity for evil. He was considering whether he should ask Izzy Bannister if he could pay a visit to Markham in prison, as his MP, to enquire after his wellbeing.

"I believe that Thames Valley police are continuing their enquiries" Mr Evans added.

Tom nodded. The proceeds of the Proton account were now lodged in an escrow account whilst the powers that be decided what to do with it. Tom imagined that it would get swallowed up by the Treasury, but that was not his concern any longer.

"So back to work then?" said Mr Evans, raising his glass. Tom reciprocated.

"We have a vote this evening then I'm going to slip away" he said as he took another sip of his whisky.

* * *

"You're just a big softie Tom!" said Georgina as she watched Tom cradling his daughter in his arms. They were in the kitchen at Shepherds Cottage. All of a sudden the house seemed very small. Naomi had taken over their guest room and mini-Scobie was sleeping with her parents.

Sid had returned to his own business, while Mike was still the duty driver in the constituency. Georgina had called ahead to say that she wouldn't mind stopping by to get an exclusive with the local MP, who had been reported as unharmed after a gangland shootout. The big story in the local news was the death of Don Johnson who had been Tom's agent.

"I'm hoping that I can finally write up the whole grisly saga, once I get legal clearance to do so" Georgina had said to Tom on the phone when they spoke.

"It'll take some explaining" he had said. "It's not a straight-forward story, and readers will lose interest."

"Ah, but we have our own hero at the centre of the story" she replied.

He sensed she was gunning for another award. Fair enough, but he would have to be careful about how his own part was told. He didn't want any glory in a story where so many people had died.

"I know he's a big softie" echoed Anna standing up carefully, "but this little softie needs changing" she said as Naomi took the baby from Tom and they went away to tend to her.

"The good news is that Sonya has been given indefinite leave to remain and she can get some work to support herself," said Tom. "That was Anna's part in the story" he added.

As he was speaking, he began to prepare the coffee pot; Georgina had signalled her willingness to have some coffee. It would allow them time to chat through how the story should be handled. As they were speaking they both heard a car draw up.

"Might need a bigger pot" Georgina said, enjoying the homely atmosphere of the small cottage.

They heard the door being opened by Naomi. Tom recog-nized Izzy Bannister's voice. She was alone; perhaps Naomi was hoping that D S Moran might be with her.

"I thought I could smell coffee" said Izzy as she walked into the room. "Don't mind if I do!"

Tom continued making the coffee like it was normal to have a Detective Inspector and an award-winning journalist in their house.

"I'll come straight to the point" Izzy said, looking at them both.

Tom and Georgina looked at each other, not quite sure what to expect.

"Charles Markham was found hanged in his cell this morning."

They were both stunned. "I thought he was on suicide watch!" said Georgina.

"He *was* on suicide watch, but his demeanour convinced the prison authorities to lessen the level of supervision."

"I suspect that he thought he could wangle a reduced sentence on appeal" mused Georgina. "He could bribe his way out of anything."

"But once the money was gone, and with Don Johnson dead, he had run out of options on that front" said Izzy. "He must have persuaded someone to get a rope into his cell...."

"The last bribe," said Tom.

47

Markham's death was the lead story on the local evening news. There was a lot of stock footage of Markham at local events and at elegant soirées with his charming wife. It was a story of a fall from grace, a local benefactor whose wealth was based on crime and blackmail.

"The wonder is that nobody picked up on the full extent of this before now" said Anna as they watched the early evening news. "Even after his arrest."

"We didn't," said Tom. "Only once Malcolm Miller decided to kill himself did this all come to light."

"I guess we had no reason to suspect," said Anna. "He didn't figure in our lives at all. Jack and Georgina were onto something" she added. "What was it that alerted them, I wonder?"

"A tip-off," said Tom. He reminded Anna that Markham's PA had been the mole inside his organization. "Like many people, she bought into the Markham fan club, but eventually she understood that he could turn against anybody if they were no longer useful. She realized that what she thought was a great adventure giving her a sense of purpose was rotten to the core."

"I guess there is no reason why the whole story can't be told now. Markham and Don are dead, so there can be no sub-judice rules on the case against them, right?" said Anna.

"I think Georgina will see to that," said Tom. "I just spoke to Matt who told me that his source, who gave us the way into the Proton account, has been transferred by his bank to New York!"

They both smiled at the irony. They watched in silence as the news story played out on the TV. There was a passing reference to the local MP who had tangled with Markham and who had been present when Donald Johnson, his former constituency agent, was gunned down. But Mr Scobie had declined to comment.

"And in other news in our region, the roadworks on the A420 look set to drag on into the New Year...." the announcer said.

"More work for the constituency office," said Tom.

* * *

"When you go home tell them of us and say,
   For your tomorrow we gave our today."

Tom stood still during the silence at the Remembrance ceremony in the market square in Wandage. How many times had he and his mates walked or cycled past the war memorial over the years. The names inscribed on it represented faded photographs and fading memories. Now he stood with the civic dignitaries waiting to lay their wreaths.

Was it the low November sun that made his eyes sting, or was it the memory of the lads who did not return from tours of duty he had been on? Robbo and Macca, still smiling and laughing in his mind's eye, forever young.

In his turn he marched up to the war memorial, paused and placed his own wreath at its foot. He bowed his head and turned to return to his place among the others. As he walked back he caught sight of Anna standing in the crowd. On such a sombre occasion she was beaming with pride; it made Tom smile momentarily until he recovered his composure.

So much had changed over the past twelve months. Now he was the local MP and, more importantly for him, he had become a father. As his gaze rested on the war memorial, he understood that it was up to him to make a difference in the world. There were other Markhams out there who needed to have their activities uncovered. To allow them to continue doing what they were doing was a betrayal of people like Jack and Georgina and Izzy, who sought to make things a little bit better for everyone.

Watching the ceremony was one man, who stood anonymously amongst the others gathered there. He too was reflecting on all of the things that had changed over the past year.

"Well, Mister Scobie" he murmured to himself, "revenge is a dish best served cold." So, saying he disappeared into the crowd as it dispersed after the ceremony.

NPW
II II 24
60,087 words

ABOUT THE AUTHOR

Nick Watts has worked in Westminster, in a variety of guises, since 1991. During this time he has seen the travails of the Major Government, the arrival of New Labour, Brexit and the subsequent political convulsions. He has worked with MPs and Peers from all of the main political parties, and has led delegations on overseas visits. He has a good understanding of the kind of people who become politicians, and the pressures they have to deal with. *Reparation* is his second book.

ALSO BY NICK WATTS

Ridgeway

Intrigue, Conspiracy and Murder...

A General Election is looming and former soldier Tom Scobie is first on the scene of a fatal road accident. It is the local MP's car. What caused it to leave the road for no obvious reason?

The vacant seat will be a shoo-in for the chosen candidate, and is therefore much sought after. But who will that be - a local insider, an A-lister from party HQ or a complete outsider?

There are dark forces at play and it rapidly becomes clear that there is much more at stake for than just normal local political shenanigans.

Tom has to discover the truth, but who can he trust? How far will others go?

Tom needs to use all his skills and guile to uncover what really is going on, and perhaps even to survive...

Printed in Great Britain
by Amazon

51891776R00142